Be the Light

Be the Light

· · · · · · ·

LIZ CRISOSTOMO

TURNING
STONE
PRESS

First published in 2012 by Turning Stone Press, an imprint of
Red Wheel/Weiser, LLC
With offices at:
665 Third Street, Suite 400
San Francisco, CA 94107
www.redwheelweiser.com

ISBN (paperback): 978-1-61852-016-6
ISBN (hardcover): 978-1-61852-015-9

Library of Congress Cataloging-in-Publication Data available
upon request

Cover design by Jim Warner

Printed in the United States of America
IBT
10 9 8 7 6 5 4 3 2 1

For my grandchildren, Kaysha, Branden,
Nick, Ariana, Courtney, Gian, Emma, and Kaili

Contents

Introduction

At some point in our lives, we ask ourselves "Why am I here?" "What is my purpose?"

These questions are prompted because at some depth of our being lie the answers.

Join in the journey of a grandmother who asked these questions and was led to a time before life in a realm that had all the answers. As you enjoy the story of two cousins who were given glimpses of this realm of Light and the lives of a brother and sister who lived there, you will gain insights and wisdom that is familiar. You are not alone on your journey and your quest for the meaning of your life begins to unfold.

I intend for you to recognize yourself in the characters portrayed here and be inspired by their strength, their courage, their laughter, and their Light along with their fears, their tears, and their pain. You will begin to understand why you have the talents that you have, where they came from, and why you have been given those gifts. Ultimately, you will re-examine those inner questions and the answers will reveal themselves.

Part I

⌕ A Journey Back in Time ⌕

KAREN WALKED OUT OF the doctor's office feeling older than her 60 years as a solitary tear rolled down her cheek. She stepped out of the building and felt the warmth of the summer day. With her eyes slightly closed, she lifted her face into the sunlight and said, "Thank you, Mr. Sun." She didn't know how this ritual began, but she had been saying "Thank you, Mr. Sun" ever since she could remember. No matter what was happening in her life, she always felt comforted by the warmth of the sun.

Karen walked slowly to the parking lot, thinking of the consultation time with Scott. Dr. Scott Newman was not only her personal physician, but he called her in to consult on some of his cases. She recalled the first time she met him when he came to intern at Lakeview General Hospital where she, Dr. Karen Campten, was head of Neurology. She instantly liked him and over the years they became good friends. She retired five years ago but was occasionally asked to consult. No matter how many patients she had helped, she always felt sad for those patients who could not be helped. This afternoon's consultation was one of those sad times.

She made it to the parking lot where her car was parked but before she could get in, she heard soft music, a melody that she had heard before. *Where is that coming from?* she wondered as she looked around. It seemed to be coming from the park nearby. She stood there and listened to the soothing music again and then headed toward the park. The music soothed her and haunted her at the same time. *I've heard that music before, somewhere back in time.* She came to the park and looked around and saw a few mothers chatting and children playing, all oblivious of the music.

"Where is that music coming from?" she asked aloud to no one in particular. She looked at the trees. As if in answer to her outspoken question, their branches were swaying in the breeze as if dancing to the beat of the music. She walked to the nearest tree and as she got closer she could definitely hear it. She looked up and no one was there, but she knew that the music was definitely coming from the branches.

I'm losing my mind, she thought, and then she laughed out loud thinking, *This is all I need on top of everything else.* She left the park and headed for her car with these haunting thoughts, *I've heard that music before. When, where?*

"Well," she said to herself, "that was a nice interruption." She started driving and headed for her cottage on the lake but could not get that music out of her mind. She knew that she had heard it before, somewhere a long time ago, but couldn't quite place it.

A half hour later, she pulled into her driveway. She entered her cozy cottage and immediately felt surrounded by all her favorite things. She made her way into the kitchen to make a cup of tea. As she prepared her tea to take to her garden, she thought of her husband, Spencer, who had died over 30 years ago. She still missed him terribly. With her cup of tea in hand she stopped long enough to take her shawl with her and walked outside to her favorite place, her garden, which she always called her "field of flowers."

It wasn't really a field, as the garden was only a small patch in her small, but easily maintained, backyard. She settled into her favorite piece of wooden lawn furniture that was now weathered but still comfortable. She sipped her tea, then placed it on the attached small table. As she put her tea cup down, she glanced over at the empty chair on the other side of the table. She would often imagine that Spencer was sitting there with her as they enjoyed the blooming flowers and the lake just beyond the garden. She knew, of course, that Spencer wasn't there, but she always felt that a loving presence was always in the garden with her. She smiled, remembering her wonderful early life with Spencer and their two daughters. He was killed in a fatal car accident when the girls were still young, and Karen ended up juggling her medical career and raising the girls alone.

Her cousin and her best friend, Brian, a marine biologist and a talented musician, helped her through those tough times. He was partially blind when she first met him. He was four years older than she was and she fell madly in love with him. She always wanted to play with him and he didn't mind. Their mothers were sisters and lived 200 miles apart, but they got together on all holidays and sometimes in between. Karen would always bring Brian flowers and tell him about their different colors. Brian could only see a blur of colors. Sometimes he would ask his little cousin to describe things for him, like the shape of the leaves on the branches. He loved being outdoors and being where the trees were.

Karen's eyes suddenly flew wide open as she remembered Brian saying, "Do you hear the music from the trees, K?"

He had always called her K. Karen knew right at that moment that she heard the same music that her cousin could hear when he was a young boy. *I've got to tell him about the trees in the park,* she thought excitedly, *maybe he'll tell me more about the music and that I'm not losing my mind. Well, maybe we have both lost our minds. I wonder if he'll still remember. After all, he's old now just like*

Be the Light

me. She laughed out loud thinking what Brian would say about the "old" remark, "Speak for yourself, I'm not old." Although he was 64 years old, he still travelled around the world, studying the mammals of the deep. He was a world renowned scientist who knew more than anyone about whales and dolphins and had written books about the behavior and the languages of our friends who lived in the ocean.

While still in medical school, Karen helped her cousin regain the full use of his eyesight through research and the use of herbs, high-tech equipment, and surgery. She learned about the various herbs and their amazing healing powers from David, a medical student and the son of a Native American shaman. Karen spent many summers and school breaks with David visiting his family on the reservation. She was loved and instantly embraced by the Native Americans. She blended right in with her long black hair and her golden brown skin, which favored her father's Pacific Islander coloring. She learned so much from David's father, the medical man on the reservation, and he was surprised at Karen's ability to quickly understand.

David was sent to medical school so that he could combine both modalities of healing. After graduation, David went back to the reservation and opened a hospital and he trained many doctors in his unorthodox way of treating patients. He and Karen still kept in touch with each other, even now in their twilight years. Karen smiled at those memories. Her knowledge of the healing herbs had helped many of her patients including Brian.

She felt her eyelids getting heavier and she knew that she was drifting off to sleep. A short nap surrounded by her flowers and her lake view was not uncommon for Karen. Then she heard the music again, the same music from the trees at the park. Without looking up at the branches of the pepper trees in her yard, she was somehow content knowing that it was coming from those branches and she just allowed the music to soothe and comfort her.

Suddenly, she sensed the presence of someone sitting in the empty chair next to her and with eyes half open, she glanced over and saw that someone was indeed sitting there smiling at her. She didn't get startled or frightened, she just smiled back. She instinctively knew that this being was not of this Earth. She didn't know how she knew, she just knew. She kept looking at him sitting there glowing and shimmering with the most beautiful lights she had ever seen. The colors were like silver and blue mingling with each other yet luminous and translucent. She just sat there staring, yet she wasn't sure if her eyes were open. She seemed to be seeing him with the eyes behind her eyes.

Am I dead? She didn't speak the words, she only thought them, but he answered her, *Do you want to be dead?* It wasn't spoken out loud. She seemed to hear it in her head.

Do I want to be dead? What kind of a question is that? No, I don't want to be dead, well . . . not yet anyway. Again, she knew she hadn't said the words but that somehow he could hear her response.

As you wish, came his answer.

Then with clarity, amazing clarity, she excitedly said out loud, "I know you!"

"*Yes, you do, I have been with you all your life,*" came the response.

This time, she knew her eyes were opened and she really looked at him. There was so much love coming from him that she felt so safe, so warm, protected, and loved. Then she felt her eyelids getting heavier and heavier again and just before she completely closed her eyes, she glimpsed two other figures standing next to her visitor.

Her breath caught in her throat. *I know you two!* Her heart felt like it was bursting with such joy and exhilaration.

"Yes, you do," answered the beautiful woman who was surrounded with so many different colors that they were twinkling like stars all around her.

"Hello, Little One," answered the man standing with the woman. He was so beautiful, so majestic look-ing, with the same twinkling lights as the woman. This time she heard their voices and she knew she had heard them before. They were so familiar, so loving.

They are the King and Queen, MY King and Queen! She was filled with so much joy she thought she would burst wide open. She smiled thinking of his words, "little one." Her father used to call her that.

"You called me that, too," she managed to say and smiled as sleep finally took over and she drifted off, still smiling.

⌒ The Flowers ⌒

T HE INCESSANT RINGING WOKE Karen up. She opened her eyes, and still trying to get her bearings, she heard the doorbell ring again. She grabbed her shawl that had fallen off her shoulder and stopped when she noticed there was a bouquet of exquisite flowers on her lap. Still trying to get fully awake, she sat back down and stared at the flowers. They were glowing, shimmering in soft luminous lights. She had never seen anything like that before.

Yes, I have, she thought. *I just had a dream about these flowers. Or was it a dream? How did these flowers get here?* Then she smiled as the dream came back in vivid clarity. *Oh my God! It wasn't a dream, I was there. I saw it all. I understand now!*

She reached for the flowers but the moment she touched them, the lights disappeared, the glow faded away. *Oh!* She was startled at first but she knew why the lights went out. She held the flowers up to her nose and inhaled their fragrance. *What a fragrance. It should be bottled.* She laughed out loud knowing that this was not possible. Just as no artist could capture the true colors of nature on his canvas, no chemist could duplicate this fragrance. With the bouquet of flowers in her hand, she finally stood up.

"Oh, there you are," Lola announced as she spotted Karen looking dazed but smiling.

"Did you take a nap out here, again? You must be getting old." They both laughed.

Lola was only a few years older than Karen and they'd known each other for many years. "Shasha is waiting for us. Are you ready to go?" Lola asked, and Karen nodded.

They climbed into the golf cart that Lola drove and made their way to Shasha's La Hacienda. "You look different," Lola observed as she looked at her friend, "You are positively glowing. Did you have a hot date that you're not telling about?"

Karen laughed and said, "No, my friend, not a hot date but the most absolutely wonderful afternoon." Before Lola could inquire about her afternoon, they arrived at the La Hacienda, a mere two-minute ride.

La Hacienda is a ten-acre, exclusive, active seniors' community that Shasha owns. Shasha, a famous model turned fashion designer, successful in her own right but having amassed a fortune from her four previous marriages, bought this beautiful piece of real estate on the lakefront. She had a hundred cottages built on the property as a residence for active seniors only. The grounds were beautifully landscaped and impeccably maintained. The big house at the heart of the property was exquisitely designed for the affluent.

There was always some kind of social activity going on. From walking or jogging on the trail around the complex, to cocktails at sunset, mimosas for Sunday brunch, croquet games, weddings parties, trip planning, and scrumptious healthy meals served in the dining room, La Hacienda was a sought after place to retire.

Lola was the creative genius behind the meals served in the dining room. Shasha snatched her away from her prestigious executive chef position at the Hyatt Regency Hotel. Shasha offered her a job at La Hacienda with residency and Lola and her husband Trevor moved onto the grounds five years ago.

It was by serendipity that an adjoining half-acre parcel became available for sale two years later and Karen purchased it and had her two bedroom cottage build. Shasha was pleased when Karen agreed to be called upon for any medical emergencies at the complex. Finally, all three friends were in one place enjoying each other's company.

Shasha was waiting for them at their favorite dining table on the terrace overlooking the lake. She stood up and greeted Karen with a hug, as she always did. As the ladies settled into their seats and awaited their first course and of course their wine, Karen lovingly looked at her beautiful friends. Shasha with her golden blonde hair and fashionable ensemble was still so strikingly beautiful. Her upkeep with the latest skin care line and occasional lifts made her look forty. Lola, petite, with her reddish hair and beautiful teeth was so pretty that she still turned heads at her age. Their weekly visits to the hair, nail, and facial salons had kept them looking so much younger than their biological age.

Karen, in contrast, with her tan skin and black hair pulled back with a hair tie or hanging loosely around her shoulders, wore very little makeup and let her natural island beauty and free spirited persona shine through. No matter how many years had gone by, they would still giggle like young girls whenever they were together.

Lola went to fetch a vase for Karen's bouquet of flowers. Shasha looked at her friend and said, "You are glowing. What have you been up too?"

Karen laughed and said, "Shasha, I've just had an extraordinary afternoon, one of those beyond this world, 'aha,' moments."

Intrigued, Shasha leaned forward, "So spill it, girl-friend, what happened?"

Karen laughed again as Lola returned with the vase. Karen put the precious gift of the flowers in the vase and the three women looked with awe at the exquisite-ness of the flowers.

"Those are beautiful, Karen. Are those from your garden?" asked Shasha.

"No," replied Karen, smiling.

As the women looked at the flowers again, Lola softly said, "I think I have seen those flowers before, somewhere, but I can't remember where." Then she and Shasha both stood up at the same time, and as they bent down to smell the flowers, they both bumped heads. They all laughed.

"Great minds think alike," Karen said, and they laughed again. As the two women inhaled the fragrance of the flowers, they both sat down and became quiet, as if in their own private thoughts.

"I know those flowers. I'm getting goose bumps," Shasha said and Lola agreed, "I'm getting goose bumps too."

As Karen watched her two dearest friends, she saw a glow around them. *This is so good.*

She barely whispered the words, "Be the Light," but Lola heard her and she reached into her pocket and said, "Look what I found when I was going through some things."

She pulled out a pin that read, "Be the Light Foundation." The other two women laughed as Lola passed the pin to them. While they sipped their wine and ate their salads, they were each in their own thoughts as they remembered that night when they all met at the gala affair of the Be the Light Foundation.

The Friendships Resume

THE THREE FRIENDS RECALLED that evening they met some 25 years ago. A gala affair was held at the Los Angeles Convention Center for six non-profit organizations to raise awareness for their causes. Brian, Karen's cousin, was scheduled to speak on saving the endangered species of the deep. Other causes included awareness of the depletion of the ozone layer, the destruction of the rain forest, and research into the cures for cancer, diabetes, and heart disease. All the notables, including celebrities, were there for this lavishly catered affair and many were writing generous checks for their favorite charity.

Karen was standing in the back of the already crowded room listening to Brian's speech about marine life and its importance to the ecological balance of the planet. He spoke about deciphering the languages of the whales and the dolphins and what they had to teach us. Spellbound at the passion in her cousin's voice as he talked of his lifelong work of protecting his friends of the deep, she didn't notice the beautiful blonde standing next to her until she spoke.

"He is very brilliant and well known for his research work," she spoke softly to Karen. Karen looked at her and recognized the famous fashion designer, Shasha. They introduced themselves and for some inexplicable reason, Karen was instantly drawn to her, as if she had known her all her life, although they didn't travel in the same circle. Shasha's second husband had known of Brian's work and had been a big supporter of the cause. That was how Shasha knew of Brian's work and continued to support his cause even after their divorce. The two women continued to chat after the speech and the applause and made their way to the buffet table.

Brian caught up with Karen and Shasha and after they congratulated him on the persuasive speech, Trevor and Jonathan joined them. Trevor and Jonathan were Brian's closest friends and they came for support. After everyone was introduced, the men left to talk to more people and Shasha and Karen settled at an empty table to enjoy their meal.

Trevor and Jonathan had been friends since high school and they both met Brian while on their spring break from college. Brian was also home for spring break and was sitting on the beach intensely concentrating on a high-tech detection gadget directed at the water's edge so he didn't notice that Trevor and Jonathan were standing there watching him.

Trevor, who was studying to be a mechanical engineer, asked, "What do you have there?"

Brian looked up and said, "Hi, I'm Brian, and this little gadget is supposed to detect the sounds of the dolphins, but I can't seem to get it to work properly."

"May I?" asked Trevor.

"Be my guest," Brian responded, relieved to hand over the gadget. They all sat down and Brian explained what the gadget was supposed to do.

Trevor studied it for a while while Jonathan introduced himself. Jonathan, who was studying political science, said, "If it's mechanical, Trevor will figure it out."

Brian explained that he was studying to be a marine biologist and home for spring break. He pointed to a huge home behind them. Trevor pushed a few buttons on the gadget but like Brian, he couldn't get it working either. "Tools, I need tools to open this up to figure it out."

"Let's go to my house; I'm sure I have some tools there," Brian invited them and they made their way to the house. There, they found the tools and it wasn't long before Trevor fixed the detection gadget. The three spent the rest of the day talking and getting to know each other. Trevor and Jonathan were fascinated as Brian explained the languages of the whales and the dolphins. They went out on Brian's dad's boat to test the detection gadget and were excited when they detected the presence of the dolphins swimming nearby. Brian continued to explain the behavior of dolphins and the music of the whales. They became fast friends and spent the rest of their spring break hanging out together.

They kept in touch with each other and shared their passions over the years. Brian and Jonathan had gone to see Trevor's act at the Improv where he moonlighted as a comedian to help pay for his tuition. During summer breaks they spent most of their time at Brian's beach house and picking up girls at the beach or throwing the football around. Brian's parents were used to seeing the three of them laughing and kidding around.

Karen got to meet Brian's new friends one summer when she came for a visit and she liked them instantly. Karen and Jonathan shared their passion for art and many times they could be seen sitting on the beach with their canvases painting the sunset scene.

Years later, these three friends still supported each other in their respective careers and causes.

A new friendship was taking form as Karen and Shasha enjoyed their meal and their conversation. Taking their glasses of wine, they went outside and that was how they met Lola. Lola was sitting on a bench, massaging her feet.

Shasha went up to her and compassionately said, "It's tough finding comfortable shoes."

"You can say that again," the pretty redhead responded. She looked up and instantly recognized fashion designer Shasha. "What do you recommend?"

Shasha immediately recommended different shoes for different occasions.

It turned out that Lola was the creative genius who catered the scrumptious foods they had just enjoyed. The conversation immediately turned to the food. Lola had been on her feet preparing to feed the 500 people who showed up.

Shasha immediately asked for Lola's business card. She could use Lola for her numerous social events. Karen and Shasha joined Lola on the bench and they chatted amicably.

By the time Brian, Trevor, and Jonathan found them, they were giggling like young girls. After introductions were made and they conversed more on the success of the evening, someone suggested they leave and find a coffee house. Lola left to make sure that everything was in order with her staff and she happily joined her new friends as they piled into Shasha's waiting limousine.

When they finally ended the long evening, everyone was excited and agreed that they would each be the light for others to shine and save the planet. It was an evening that all of them would remember. New and old friends bonded and a love relationship between Lola and Trevor bloomed into a happy marriage.

The three women reminisced about that night 25 years ago and agreed that it was destined to happen. They raised their wine glasses and all three happily cheered, "No such thing as a coincidence!"

Throughout the meal, Karen lovingly watched her friends as she recalled what had happened that afternoon in her field of flowers. She wasn't ready to share her extraordinary afternoon until she spoke to Brian. She then reached for the flowers in the vase and carefully split them into three smaller bouquets and gave one to each instructing them to place the flowers somewhere close so they could see them every day when they awoke. The ladies said their goodnights and hugged and Lola drove Karen back to her cottage.

After putting her now smaller bouquet of flowers in a vase, she noticed that she was still holding the Be the Light Foundation pin. She looked at it again and smiled at how they were led to be together again, an agreement they all made not so long ago in another place and another time. They all agreed to "Be the Light." Little did they know that this was their mission.

Karen laughed and laughed so hard she felt happy tears on her face. She placed the vase of flowers on her nightstand. *Perfect place, right next to me as I sleep.* Karen was unaware that right at that precise moment, Shasha and Lola were also placing their flowers on their nightstands.

Karen then settled in and placed a call to Brian. He answered almost immediately. "Hey K, I was just thinking of you." Karen smiled. "Listen, Brian are you going to be in town in the next couple of days? I'd like to come to the beach house and hang out with you. Is this okay with your schedule? It's rather important that I talk to you."

"Sure K, come by. Are you all right? Did something happen?" Brain asked.

Karen responded happily, "I am great, Brian, better than great. I'll tell you all about it when I see you in a couple of days. How about having lunch ready and I'll be there around noon the day after tomorrow?" Brian agreed and they said goodnight. Karen hung up and smiled.

Goodnight, Prince Branigi, she thought. She then looked at her exquisite, out of this world flowers, smiled, and said, *goodnight Shajula, goodnight Brilola.*

Sometime in the middle of the night, the flowers in their respective places began to fill up the room with their glow and the three women, deep in sleep, were smiling.

⤙ The Prince and the Princess ⤚

O N THE HOUR DRIVE to her cousin's beautiful home on the beach, Karen thought of all that had happened before she heard the music in the park. She thought about her cousin Brian, her best friend, and all he had been through on his journey, and all that they had been through since they were children. She thought of the beautiful beach home that she was headed to and reminisced on the wonderful times she spent there growing up and the memories she had of her own children spending many summers and school breaks there.

Her uncle Ed, a science professor, and her Aunt Teri, a musician and music teacher, had always opened their home to Karen and her young children. They loved the constant activity and noise.

When her beloved aunt passed on, Brian was in the middle of an unpleasant divorce from his wife, Monique. Distraught by the death of his mother and the breakup of his marriage, Brian moved into the beach house to be with his father and gave Monique the condo in the city.

It was a hard year for Brian; he only saw his then ten-year-old son, Chase, every other weekend because of the custody arrangement, and he had to care for his dad, who was already showing signs of Alzheimer's. A year later, Uncle Ed passed on and Brian grieved again. Karen was there during this hardship. Brian and his family had been there for her when she had also lost both her parents in a tragic auto accident just five years earlier. Brian was there for her when her husband Spencer died. Both cousins endured the worst and the best of times.

Now, Brian was still at the beach house enjoying the quiet and the solitude, the ideal place for continuing his research and even more ideal for composing his music, his two passions. Karen smiled, *He truly has fulfilled his mission to "be the Light" in the world of shadows.*

Brian greeted her at the door and she gave him a big hug. "You are positively glowing!" Brian announced as he held her at arm's length and took a good look at his cousin. "What's up, K, a new man in your life?"

Karen laughed and said "No, no new man in my life, just in love with being alive." After she settled her overnight bag in the guest room, she placed her most recent precious commodity, her vase of flowers, on the dining table and joined Brian in the kitchen where a glass of white wine was waiting for her and she helped him carry his famous seafood salad to the table.

Brian talked about his recent trip to the Bahamas with a group of scientists who were studying the behavior of the marine life there. They then talked about the children and the grandchildren and how they were all doing. Brian kept looking at the flowers that Karen had placed on the table. "Where did you say you got those flowers?" he asked.

"I didn't say," Karen responded with a twinkle in her eye.

Brian reached out, started to turn the vase slowly, and observed, "It's interesting how the light shines on the petals and they act like a prism, refracting the lights all around. Do you see it?"

"Yes, I do, but it's not like a prism, refracting light, it's more like the light is coming from within the petals and is reflecting outward. Look closer."

Brian looked closer and said. "Nah, it's refracting the lights."

Karen laughed, "If you say so, Proffy." She started calling her cousin "Proffy" when he was a professor teaching marine biology at the university.

After they cleared away the lunch dishes, they took their freshly brewed coffee out to the terrace to enjoy the ocean view. "So what is really going on with you, K?" Brian looked closely at his cousin, remembering that she said she wanted to talk about an important matter.

Karen leaned back on her chair and took a deep breath. "Do you still hear music from the trees?" she asked.

Before Brian could answer, Karen continued, "I heard it too, the other day, first at the park, then in my garden, and I know where we first heard it."

Brian stared at Karen, shocked at what he had just heard. He had always thought that he was the only person who could hear the music from the trees. He first heard it when he was a young boy and to this day, he still could hear it. He didn't talk about it anymore to anyone. He tried as hard as he could to re-create the same music, but he was never successful. He even took a tape recorder once to record the sounds, but whenever he pushed the Record button the music would stop. Now he just simply enjoyed the soothing music.

Karen then told Brian about being in the garden, the appearance of the apparitions, and then how she fell asleep. "Brian, I saw where we came from, our beginnings before we came into this life. It was a wonderfully happy place of lights. Thousands of different colors of light are like nothing seen here. There is music from the trees and flowers and even music from the mountains and the oceans. Music like I heard in the park and in my garden and I know it's the same music you hear. We were beings of Light and everything there is beautiful beyond words."

Brian lean forward, fascinated at what he was hearing, and he was getting goose bumps all over.

Karen explained that the Light Beings there were on a mission to help those who were here. Karen was excited to finally tell someone about what she saw and she didn't want to miss anything. Every time Brian wanted to interrupt to ask a question or to clarify what she was saying, Karen would raise her hand, signaling Brian to hold on until she was through relating everything.

"We learned all about the life in this place before we came here. We were shown how the people here on Earth lived and we saw the struggle and conflict that come from shadows that encircle this planet. We were shown the wars, the sickness, the pain, the greed, the despair and desperation, and not just what the people do to themselves and to each other, but also to the planet."

She explained that some Light Beings chose to remain and help us from there and some chose to put on the human form and make the journey here to fulfill a heroic mission to bring more Light into this world.

"But, sadly, many who have come here have forgotten that they came here for a purpose. We remember our mission when we first get here and then we get so immersed in the Shadow that surrounds us and we forget. But we are not forgotten because the Light Beings from the other place are constantly helping us. Some of us wake up and rise above the Shadow and some of us continue to live in the Shadow. Don't you see, Brian, you and I have always known that we have a purpose for our lives and our being and now it has become so clear for me what our purpose is, what everyone's mission is!"

Karen finally stopped talking and waited for Brian's reaction. He sat back and stared at his cousin in amazement and was aware that he was still getting goose bumps all over his body.

"Well, that is one fantastic dream, K," was all that Brian could say as he still stared at her. Somehow, he didn't know how, this place of lights she had described sounded so familiar to him. Karen got up and returned with the vase of flowers and she placed the vase on the table in front of them.

"I found a bouquet of these flowers on my lap when I woke up or came to and Brian, they were glowing with those luminous colors that I saw in that place. They came from the field of flowers. When I touch them, the lights went off. That's why I said they were not refracting the light, they were the Light."

Brian stared at the flowers, touched their petals, and was very quiet as he gazed out at the ocean thinking about the fantastic "story" he had just heard.

"You were transported there, somehow, weren't you?" Brian asked very quietly.

"I believe I was." Karen replied, silently grateful that her cousin didn't laugh at her.

She watched him quietly gazing at the ocean and she described their time together as Light Beings.

"Brian," Karen said softly, "we were brother and sister in that life. We had the most wonderful and happy life. We were actually a prince and a princess. We were the royal children of the rulers, the King and Queen. You were Prince Branigi and I always called you Gi."

Brian suddenly started laughing. He laughed so hard, he had to hold his sides.

"K, you are so right. When you were little, you called me 'glee.' Our mothers couldn't figure out how you came up with that name, but you kept calling me 'glee.' I guess you were trying to say Gi."

Karen joined in the laughter. She had a vague recollection of using the nickname.

Karen continued to tell Brian about their lives as the royal children and all their favorite things to do. When Karen told Brian that he called his pet dolphin, Sergie, Brian laughed again.

"My mother told me that when I first learned to walk, I would walk to the beach and call out 'Sergie.' They would run after me and stop me from walking right into the water. I guess I was looking for my dolphin. Now I'm beginning to understand my affinity for dolphins."

Brian then came up with questions and Karen explained what she saw when they were children and how they each came to the decision to leave that happy magical place.

They talked until it was time for dinner and they dressed to have dinner at their favorite place along the beach. They walked arm in arm along the beach and stopped to gaze at the magnificent sunset that covered the whole sky.

"What a beautiful sunset. It just takes your breath away." Brian commented.

Karen had a far away look in her eyes as she also gazed at the beautiful artwork and said so softly, "A young child and a palette of colors with the help of a winged horse could paint that."

Brian gave his cousin a quizzical look but before he could question her soulful remark, they arrived at the restaurant. During dinner Karen showed Brian the pin and they laughed again and talked about that night and how the six friends came together as they had promised.

Brian asked, "How are we, those who have forgotten our origin, supposed to remember that we are Light Beings?"

Karen recalled the words of the King and Queen on the mountaintop. "We are constantly given reminders, every day of our lives. The sunset we just saw with the different colors of light, the sunrise in the morning, even the stars at night. You said so yourself, *it takes your breath away.* That is joy that comes from inside of you, that part of you that you always are, a being of Light. It was explained that the reason we come as a newborn baby is being an infant triggers the joy that is within. An infant is a new creation being witnessed by all. When you look at an infant, your heart smiles first, then your face smiles. It's the same way when we see a little kitten or a puppy or even a new blossom. It's a new creation and we smile from the joy we feel inside. We are here to experience the joy that is the Light itself.

"When we experience fear, a shadow surrounds us and it's that shadow that makes us forget that we are Light."

Brian thought for a while and then said, "Well, that's simple enough if we remember that Light will take away the Shadow, but many people today live in that fear lifestyle. They are traumatized by events that occurred; they are worried about surviving in this world of opposites. If everyone remembered that they were beings of Light, then what would there be to fear?"

"Exactly!" Karen exclaimed excitedly. "That is what each one of us is here to do, to be a light in the world so that everyone's Light will come through. That is what the mission is for those in the Kingdom of Light. They are constantly reminding us to 'be the Light.' We live in a world of opposites, but we can live harmoniously with the Shadow, if we remember that the Shadow itself is only fleeting and the Light is forever. Then and only then will we know that there is nothing to fear from this world because we are not of this world, we are of the Kingdom of Light."

Brian said, "But how do we remember and change our lifestyle of living in fear?"

Karen again recalled and repeated the words of the King and Queen on the mountaintop, "*Throughout your journey in the smaller kingdom, you will be given reminders of who you are. You will be guided to meet someone who will* be a teacher of the light, or you will be given a book to read or attend an event that stirs the memory of the place you are from. When you go within to that place of silence, you will hear our voices and you will remember who you truly are and there you shall find the joy, the bliss, the love, and the peace that you've always had because it is who you are and that will never change. When you feel lost in the midst of the Shadow, remember that it is outside of you, it is not who you are, you are not a being of the Shadow, the Shadow is fleeting, it is temporary. You are a Light Being and the Light is within waiting for you to bring it forth to dispel the Shadow and shine forth, expanding and touching all those around you."

Karen continued, "Brian, all though our lives, we get glimpses of the joy, the love and peace, and we can't explain where it comes from, or we get a moment of bliss that is inexplicable but only lasts for a short while. These are the reminders, those quiet moments when we contemplate and reflect on all that has happened, we feel that peace, we experience that bliss. Some of us are open to remember earlier and some of us remember at the end of our journey. I have seen that look of peace when my patients make their transition from this physical world into the next world. All the worrying from the fear just vanishes and they look so happy and peaceful. They remembered who they are and what they are all about, they finally see, in that moment, how profoundly simple it all is. We make it complicated with our choices."

Brian said, "I do remember those times of peace and bliss, Karen, especially when I hear the music of the whales and the dolphins. It's like being in another world and I'm always drawn to it in those moments when I feel somewhat lost or grieving, like when I was going through my divorce or when Mom and then Dad died. I would take my boat out and look for the dolphins and I would feel at home somehow. Those may be the moments when I would return to the Light and the Shadow would disappear. I see now that connecting to that Light within me makes all the pain, suffering, and confusion fade away."

Karen smiled remembering her times of peace and bliss whenever she was painting or helping a patient heal their chronic pain or when she was just sitting in her field of flowers enjoying their beauty and the peaceful tranquility of the lake. But even when she remembered those moments, it still did not even come close to that amazing feeling of peace and bliss that she was given a glimpse of the other day.

When they returned to the house, Karen once again split the flowers and put Brian's share in a vase and told him to place it on his nightstand and she took her now smaller bouquet into the guest room as she prepared for bed.

That night the flowers glowed and their light filled both rooms while the cousins smiled in their sleep.

The next morning Brian excitedly told Karen that he had a dream about the Kingdom of Light. Karen had told him that the other place was called the Kingdom of Light and the Light Beings there called the Earth the Kingdom of Opposites where both the Light and the Shadow exist.

He said he saw Sergie and was playing with him in the water just like the good old days. Then Brian said something that completely took Karen by surprise and confirmed that he did indeed remember the "good old days" that came to him in a dream.

"Karen, you didn't tell me about your own pet horse, Wings. I saw you flying around with Wings. I also saw your sunflowers and know how they came about. I also saw the sunset painting. Now I know what you meant last night, about how a young child with the help of a winged horse can paint a magnificent sunset. Why didn't you tell me about that? Didn't you also see that?"

"Of course, I saw that, Brian, but I wanted to tell you about you and how you took your passion for the whales, the dolphins, and the music with you into this lifetime. I guess I wanted to make sure you understood your mission here, or rather everyone's mission." Karen explained.

Brian smiled lovingly at his cousin, "I do understand, PK."

Karen reached over and hugged her cousin; he *did* remember the "good old days." Karen was given the nickname "PK" by the King; it was short for Princess Karicoma, and only those in the Kingdom of Light used that name.

The cousins were in good spirits that morning. They now completely understood why they were meant to be together in this lifetime. Brian asked, "I wonder why we are being shown this now? The King told us on the mountaintop that we would see bits and pieces of the kingdom on our journey here, but this seems to be more than bits and pieces, a lot more, like the whole thing. Why do you think this is so, K?"

Karen smiled as if she had a secret. With eyes twinkling, she responded, "I think it's because we need to tell the grandchildren about the Kingdom of Light. They are, after all, the future leaders of this world and we need to remind them to 'be the Light' in the world."

"Hmm, maybe, but I think there is something else happening here. But telling the grandchildren is an excellent idea. What about our children, shouldn't they also know about it? And what about our friends, wouldn't they also like to know that we made a pact with them and it came true?"

"I have been thinking a lot about our grandchildren lately, and I want them to know about their Light, about our Light, and who we all are. I think that what is happening here is that we are shown all this so we can tell our grandchildren and then they in turn can tell theirs. I feel that we have shown our children what we know about life and have planted those seeds within them. Now we have a chance to plant new seeds with our grandchildren because we now have this truth of where we came from and why we are truly here. Our children and grandchildren and their will be the ones to make a difference in this world of opposites. I have been feeling so strongly about doing something or leaving behind something for the grandchildren about the wisdom I've gained in this journey of life and this was when all this started happening. I am being guided to let them know the truth. Don't you see that, Brian? As for our friends, they will know soon enough."

Karen told Brian that since she had this revelation, she had made notes about the Kingdom of Light and sent it to her good friend, Gail, from Simon Publishing Company. Gail called and said it would make a good children's book and she, was going to work with Karen's notes to start putting the story together.

Karen said, "Gail thinks that we can get it ready for publication in time for the holidays. I want this to never be forgotten, which is why I want it in print to be passed down through generations. Would you help me plan when this will happen and how we will tell them?"

Brian acquiesced and the cousins began making plans. They decided to have the grandchildren at the beach house for a weekend to celebrate Karen's birthday. Since Karen's birthday was only two months away, they spent the rest of the morning making plans.

When Karen was leaving for her drive home, she hugged her cousin and was happy that she had shared her experience with him. They had both changed in the last 24 hours.

As she turned to leave, Karen asked Brian with a twinkle in her eye, "By the way, do you ever wonder why you started calling me K? Think maybe it's short for PK instead of Karen?"

Brian laughed, "No, it's short for 'kilowatt.' Be the Light, K!" and he waved goodbye as she got into her car.

Karen drove home smiling and making mental plans for how she could get all their grandchildren together in the next two months. She was happy and knew that Brian was too now that they had been given a glimpse of who they were and where they came from.

She recalled the many conversations that she and Brian had had over the years. At every crisis they each faced, they would say, *There was a reason why this happened; what am I supposed to learn here?* The answers they came up with were never too far from the truth.

Karen reminisced about all she'd been through in this life with all the twists and turns, the shadows that came with the tragedies, the loss of both her parents, the failed first marriage, the tragedy ending the second marriage, the unwise choices in her younger years, yet throughout all that, she always felt a loving presence with her. She also recalled the many times when she was guided out of danger, or guided to be at certain places, to meet certain people, to be at the right place at the right time, just as the King and Queen had told them would happen. *Everything happens in its divine order. It's not about understanding why and how things and events happen but in trusting that we are never alone and we are always guided, protected, and led to our highest good on the journey.*

"No such thing as a coincidence," she and Brian would always say. Now she truly understood why these things all happened just as they did. It was all part of reminding her of her mission. She laughed out loud. She had so much to share with her grandchildren.

Brian sat on his terrace gazing out at the ocean and recalling the events of the day before. He was also recalling his battle with the Shadow, and like Karen, he also concluded, *there is no such thing as a coincidence.* He called his son, Chase and asked to have the grandchildren, Corina and Jo, for Karen's birthday weekend. Chase agreed.

ꜿ A Grandmother's Wish Ꜿ

W ITH ONLY A FEW more miles until she reached home, Karen thought of her children and the beautiful grandchildren they had given her. Her oldest daughter, Elaine, who owned and operated a small but successful gift store, had two children: Shane, now 17 and in his last year of high school, with plans to study architecture in college, and her daughter Lee, now 9 years old.

Karen's other daughter, Rosemarie, a vice principal in the local high school, gave her two more grandchildren. Her first granddaughter Kay, now 19, studies law, and 15-year-old Nigel, a star basketball player, has high ideals and hopes to get into politics and change the condition of the world. Karen smiled to herself, thinking of her four grandchildren and how their talents were coming forth. Their Light would shine brightly.

Brian's son Chase has two daughters, Corina, 14, who used to want to be a singer and now wanted to be a journalist and be in front of a camera reporting the news, and 8-year-old Jo, who displayed musical talent.

Karen placed a call to her oldest grandchild, Kay. "Hey, G-ma, what's up?" Kay's cheery voice came on.

Kay was the first to call Karen "grandma" and somewhere along the way, "grandma" had become "G-ma." Karen explained the plans for the weekend at Brian's beach house to celebrate her birthday and have a cousins' reunion with Brian's grandchildren.

"Sounds like fun. Hanging out at Uncle Brian's beach house is always a fun getaway from work or school." Karen's grandchildren have lovingly given Brian the honorary title of 'uncle' and Brian's grandchildren also gave Karen the honorary title of 'aunt'.

Karen asked Kay to bring Nigel and she agreed. Karen also told Kay that she'd call her mother, Rosemarie, and let her in on the plans. They talked a little more and then they said their goodbyes.

Next, Karen called her oldest grandson, Shane. She smiled as she talked to him and remembered his beautiful hazel eyes and his disarming smile that earned him the title of "hottie" in school. Shane was just as happy to take a break and hang out at the beach house and see his cousins again. He agreed to bring his sister, Lee. Karen told Shane that she'd let his mother know about the plans.

Karen then decided to drop in and visit her oldest child, Elaine, at *Remember When*, her store where you could find restored old jewelry or memorabilia. Elaine's store was only a few miles out of her way and Karen decided she'd see if Elaine was free for lunch.

When Karen arrived at her daughter's store, she was impressed with the new items she had on display. Elaine loved shopping at antique stores to find those rare pieces of the past for her customers. She also sold her own creative arts and crafts. "The past and the present all in one store," Elaine would always say.

Karen was greeted enthusiastically by her granddaughter, Lee, a permanent fixture at the shop from the time she was toddler. Now Lee went there every day after school and helped her mother run the business. Lee was a lovely child, so full of life and love of beautiful things. She especially loved pretty shoes, and even if they were too big for her, she would still walk around in them and she often wore a hat that was way too big and way too old for her. The customers enjoyed the fashion show when they came into the shop.

Elaine agreed to lunch and closed the shop, and the three of them walked to the nearby café for lunch. Karen explained her plans for a birthday reunion weekend at Brian's beach house. As if on cue, Elaine protested about not being included. Karen knew she would get resistance from her daughter and she was prepared to be calm and explain that she wanted to spend quality time with her grandchildren and that it was an opportunity to have a cousins' reunion with Brian's grandchildren.

Elaine, perceptive as usual, immediately asked, "Is there something you are not telling us?" The barrage of questions were answered in Karen's calm bedside manner. "Everything is fine, dear. The birthday weekend is just a 'grandmother's wish'; Shane already agreed to hang out with us and he said he'll bring Lee. Besides that, the following week will be Thanksgiving and we will all get together then at Rosemarie's place."

Reassured that her mother was fine, and it was probably a "senior" thing, Elaine finally agreed and they all enjoyed a lovely lunch together.

Karen pulled into her driveway an hour later, and placed her last call to Rosemarie; unlike her sister, Elaine, she thought it was a great idea for a grandparents' and grandchildren's weekend time. Rosemarie knew that the whole family would be together the following week and she would hear all about their time at the beach house then.

There was a note from Shasha and Lola posted on her front door that read, *Come by when you get in.* As soon as she unpacked, she went to La Hacienda wondering what the summons was all about.

Shasha greeted her with a tight hug, "Oh! We've been waiting for you to come home. I wanted to call you on your cell phone, but Lola said to wait until you came home. We have sooooo much to tell you."

"Hey, I've only been gone for two days. What's going on? You're acting like I've been gone forever."

Lola came rushing out of the kitchen and she also gave Karen a tight hug.

"All right already, what's going on?" Karen asked, puzzled at the behavior of her two dearest and closest friends.

The women went out on the terrace and Lola asked the busboy to bring them some coffee. "We've had the most incredibly amazing dreams the past two nights and they were identical dreams," Shasha began.

Lola continued, "Karen, we both dreamed about those flowers you gave us. The three of us were playing in the most beautiful field of flowers and there were lights, magnificent lights everywhere, and colors, so many different colors."

Shasha jumped in and exclaimed, "There were colors and lights everywhere, Karen, and we were those colors and lights and when we moved the colors move with us like a dance. It was so beautiful, it was breathtaking, like nothing I've ever seen before, but it felt like I knew the place, like I've been there before."

When Shasha stopped to catch her breath, Lola immediately jumped in, "Karen, we were making these crowns of flowers and we were dancing and chasing butterflies and we were painting different colors on the butterflies. There was also a beautiful white horse with wings and you called him 'Wings' and we went riding and flying with him all over the place."

Karen just stared at her two friends, listening and turning from one to the other as they excitedly talked about the identical dreams they had. *They are remembering the "good old days" as Brian called it. It must be the flowers! The flowers triggered something in their memory.*

Karen remembered the King explaining, *"There will be moments on your journey when you will remember this place. It only happens when the mind is quiet and you will see this place in your mind's eye and you will know that you've been here before, or the memories will come to you in a dream.*

Then Karen started laughing, laughing so hard, she was holding her sides. Shasha and Lola just stared at her.

"What's so funny?" they both asked.

"I had the same dream myself." Karen finally said after she stopped laughing.

Then they all laughed and started talking at the same time. Karen knew that the field of flowers was all that the women saw, but she felt sure that little by little, more of the kingdom would reveal itself to them. She didn't share what she had shared with Brian. She wasn't sure why she didn't, but she just knew that it would reveal itself when the time was right.

"Another thing," Lola said. "I woke up and saw the flowers you gave us glowing with the same colors that were in my dream and when I touched them, the glowing stopped. Where did you get those flowers, Karen?"

"I found them on my lap that afternoon you came and found me in the backyard waking up from a nap. That was when I had that dream about running through the field of flowers with the two of you. They just appeared right there on my lap and they were also glowing until I touched them. The dream was so real that I manifested those flowers, I guess. You read about things like that happening, don't you? I don't know, but there they are, glowing flowers not of this world." Karen hoped that her casual explanation would stop the questioning of the origin of the flowers.

"Well, whether you manifested them or someone gave them to you and you're not telling, they are sitting on my nightstand beautifying my bedroom." Shasha said.

"They are on my nightstand too," Lola said. "Maybe that was what inspired the dreams, and what beautiful dreams. I just know, I don't know how I know, but I just *know* that I've been there in that field and it does exist somewhere."

Shasha and Karen both agreed that they felt the same way. The women talked about their mutual love for butterflies and wondered if that was because of what they saw in their dreams, or was it just a coincidence?

"No such thing as a coincidence!" they said in unison as they raised their coffee cups and laughed again.

Lola said that her husband, Trevor, also had a wonderful dream that night. "He didn't dream of a field of flowers but said that he also dreamed about being in a place filled with different colors of light but that he dreamed about being in the ocean that sparkled like different colors of light and that he and two friends were playing and riding on the backs of dolphins throwing around a football."

Shasha said, "Well, that figures, we dream about flowers and the men dream about sports."

Karen just stared at Lola, shocked at what she was hearing. Then she sat back and smiled. *This was so amazing. They were all beginning to remember just like the King said they would. This was what bliss was, to remember who they were and from there grow in the Light.*

The next few weeks Karen was busy. She met with Gail from the publishing house several times. She also made a trip to the reservation to meet with David. She always enjoyed her time with David. The two like-minded friends talked for hours and she joined him while he was making his rounds in the hospital. She was always inspired by his wisdom in the healing arts. She also talked with Brian several times about the birthday plans and other matters.

The birthday weekend finally arrived, along with six grandchildren with ages from 8 to 19. The two grandparents found themselves in the midst of a lot of noise, activity, hugs, and laughter. The cousins were happy to see other and they came prepared to have fun.

They all made their way down to the beach with the barbecue grill for the hot dogs and hamburgers, the beach pails for the young girls, and the volleyball for the older kids. The cousins started the volleyball game, Lee and Jo happily started building their sandcastle, and Brian fired up the grill. The activities had begun.

After the volleyball game, the cousins had their chance to get caught up with the goings-on in their individual lives. Kay talked to Shane about college days, Nigel and Corina talked about their schools and what they were doing, and of course they all talked about music. Everyone brought out their favorite tunes and took turns playing them on the player that Brian had on hand that always came out when the kids got together.

Karen sat in her beach chair and wistfully watched the grandchildren play and laugh with each other while Brian took care of the grill. She first focused her attention on Kay, now grown into a beautiful young woman. She remembered the day she was born and how blessed she felt when she became a grandmother. She had felt her heart expand and was amazed to realize that the heart could hold so much love for this newborn baby. Kay was her first grandchild, and her first experience of another dimension of unconditional love. Kay was born a leader with an inquisitive mind. She always wanted to know why things were the way they were and how they could be changed for the better. It was no surprise that she was drawn to the law. Karen remembered the moment when Rosemarie handed her over and Karen felt the presence of Spencer standing next to her as they both gazed at this beautiful baby.

Karen smiled when Kay stopped playing volleyball to help Jo and Lee with their unsuccessful attempt to build a sandcastle. She was showing the young girls how to do it right. Her eyes suddenly filled with tears, *Kay must fully understand what we are about to tell them and she will have to keep them all in line with their purpose.*

She turned her attention to next grandchild, Shane. He and Nigel were now at the grill helping Brian. Shane, the "hottie," was so popular in high school with the girls and was always clowning around. Karen remembered his love of Lego toys when he was just a toddler. He would spend hours and hours putting those pieces together, taking them apart, and putting them back together again to take another form. It was no wonder that architecture was his calling. His creative talent, much like that of his mother, Elaine, was going to be a bright light in the world. Karen's heart opened wide as she looked at him. Shane was the great equalizer in the family. He knew how to make them laugh each time and the younger grandchildren and cousins always want to be around him.

Next, Karen looked at Nigel. Nigel had such a sweet smile with dimples. He had dark hair, dark eyes, and beautiful olive skin just like his mother, Rosemarie. Born a leader just like his cousin Kay, Nigel was president of the student council and the star basketball player for his school team. He was now beginning to show interest in music and dance as well. He was a multitalented young man with a serious side for life. His interest in political science would expand as he grew into his own gifts and talents.

Karen's tears were now flowing as her heart expanded and she smiled looking at her two grandsons. She was so proud of these young men knowing that they would grow into their talents for the world to see.

Karen could hear laughter coming from the sand-castle building group. Kay was teaching the two young girls and laughing along with them. Karen looked at her youngest grandchild, Lee. What a lovely, delightful child she was growing into. She was so girly and had enjoyed dressing up as soon as she started walking. She had a unique fashion sense and chose what she wanted to wear to school, and sometimes that meant a power struggle with her mother, Elaine. Her mother gave in most of the time, allowing Lee to express her own sense of style, or maybe Lee just wore her mother down. Lee adored her big brother, Shane, and always wanted to tag along with him and was always doing whatever it took to get his attention. Shane, a loving older brother, was never annoyed with her persistence to play; he was always patient with her because he knew that he would be leaving for college soon and he would miss her.

Karen wiped her tears away and felt her heart break-ing. She wished that Spencer was here with her watching the grandchildren playing with each other. She swal-lowed the lump in her throat as she remembered reading somewhere that if the heart breaks, it simply means that it is opening wide to give and receive more light.

Corina, Brian's granddaughter, came to join the giggling girls at the sandcastle. Corina was Brian's first grandchild and Karen truly believed that Corina's appearance in Brian's life was the powerful healing force that her cousin needed at that time in his life. Brian grieved during the separation from his son, Chase, when he and Monique went their separate ways. He went from seeing and loving his son daily to seeing him only every other weekend. He felt that he watched him grow from a distance. When Chase went away to college in San Diego, he came and stayed with his dad at the beach house every school break and spent many long hours boating with his dad. Brian always cleared his speaking engagements on those days when he knew Chase would be home with him. While Chase was proud of his father's achievements and his passion for his causes, he himself was drawn to the business world where he now owned and operated his own successful brokerage house with his wife Myrna.

When Corina was born, Brian experienced that new level of unconditional love that Karen did with Kay. Corina had expressed her love and passion for music since she was old enough to join her grandfather on the piano bench. She had a beautiful singing voice, like him, and soon developed her talent in speaking. Journalism was where she wanted to go with her persuasive speaking gift.

Jo, the youngest of Brian's grandchild, came into the world with large brown eyes, and she was extremely shy at first. She was not as animated as her cousin Lee; she observed intently and smiled to herself as if she knew a secret that no one knew about. Karen watched her nieces with love and joy, silently thanking them for the blessing that they were to her cousin's life.

These six grandchildren—sisters, brothers, and cousins—had bonded since they were born and would continue to do so for many years to come. Again, Karen felt the tears rolling down her cheek. She wiped her tears away and closed her eyes and tilted her face toward the sun, knowing its warmth would dry her wet cheeks so no one would see her crying.

She opened her eyes and saw all six grandchildren looking at her. She smiled at them, feeling her heart expanding once again as she mentally brought all of them into her heart space of love. "It's time to eat," they told her, and together they made their way to the table and enjoyed the hot dogs and hamburgers.

That evening, after they all had Uncle Brian's delicious spaghetti dinner, Karen gathered the grandchildren around and told them that instead of a movie night, she and Brian would tell them a wonderful story about a magical place.

They made popcorn and each grandchild found a comfortable place to settle in for their story time. Karen and Brian sat in a couple of comfortable over-stuffed chairs and faced the young Light Beings as they eagerly waited. For a brief moment Karen saw glimpses of lights behind the grandchildren and saw apparitions of beautiful Light Beings smiling at her and Brian. *They are the Angees.* She saw the King and Queen for a brief moment as if they were giving their approval. Then the lights disappeared.

She quickly looked at Brian and from the expression on his face, she knew that he had seen them too. He reached over and squeezed her hand to let her know. Smiling, Karen looked lovingly at their audience of the six of the most important people in their lives and began the story of the magical Kingdom of Light.

Part II

The Magical Kingdom of Light

KAREN TOOK A DEEP breath and began the tale.
*There is a magical kingdom, not far from here. It is
ruled by a very powerful and wise King, along with a very
kind and gentle Queen. The King and Queen have two children, Prince Branigi and his younger sister, Princess Karicoma, whom the King lovingly nicknamed PK. Soon after,
the Princess became known throughout the kingdom as PK.*

*Everywhere you look in this place, you see lights of differ-
ent colors. There are thousands of lights not seen anywhere
else. Everyone and everything is filled and surrounded by a
soft glow of their own special color of light. The people in
this kingdom are called Light Beings and this place is called
the Kingdom of Light. It is from these lights that the magical
power comes. Some beings are surrounded by just one color
of light, some have two or more.*

*The King and Queen are the only ones who are sur-
rounded by many colors and the lights that glow around
them twinkle like millions of stars. The Prince and Princess
also have lights that twinkle like stars but they do not have*

as many as the King and Queen. Each year they glow and twinkle with another new light color until one day they will each be surrounded with as many colors as the King and Queen and will also possess the same magical powers as the King and Queen.

Karen looked at Brian and he continued the tale.

Everyone in this magical place is happy. There are no wars here. There is no sickness or pain. It is never too hot or too cold. The sky is a blue and silver color. You can see millions and millions of stars in the night sky. The stars seem so close you can almost reach up and touch them.

There are many forests filled with trees and plants of every kind and size. Some glow with a golden color, some glow in bright orange lights, and some glow with different colors of green and blue. The forest is never dark. If you listen closely, you could hear music coming from the trees and plants. When the branches sway in the breeze, they seem to be dancing to the music.

There are fields of flowers everywhere, all glowing in different colors. They also have their own music. They too seem to be dancing to their music as they sway in the gentle breezes. When they are dancing with the breezes, they open their petals and release their own special fragrances. PK and her friends love playing in the flower fields as they pick the glowing flowers for their hair. You hear their laughter as they chase after the colorful butterflies.

There is a special part of the forest where all the animals live and roam free. Each animal glows with a soft orange and blue color. From the smallest to the largest animal, they all get along with each other. There is no need to fight for boundaries because the place is so big. There is no need to fight for food because food is plentiful.

All the children in the kingdom love to play in the forest. They swing from the vines with the monkeys or ride on the backs of elephants and lions.

There are many oceans here filled with every kind of marine life. They glow with the different colors of blue, green, and silver making the whole ocean glow and sparkle like millions of diamonds. The Prince and his friends love coming here to ride and swim with the dolphins.

There are mountains of every size here. If you get close to them, you can also hear their music as they stand glowing and majestic as if they are protecting this magical place.

There are many birds of every kind and every size that live here. From the songbirds that happily sing their songs to the eagles that soar far and high.

Brian paused waiting to get a response from their audience. The grandchildren began talking at the same time. "Is that it?", "What happened to the prince?", "What happened to the princess?", "Tell us about the dolphins," "Did they really play with the lions and the elephants?"

Karen and Brian burst out laughing. They had gotten their attention! It was exactly what they both wanted to achieve and they were pleased and Karen smiled as she continued where Brian left off.

There are millions of Light Beings who live in the magical kingdom. There are towns and cities there, just like here, filled with stores and shops. The Royal children and their friends have their favorite shops and stores. Mari from the Sweets Shoppe, one of their favorites, calls on the Royal children and their friends to come and sample her new creations of sweet bread, cookies, cakes, and candies. The children eagerly tell her which ones are their favorites.

Another favorite shop of the children is the Toy and Gadget Shoppe. Hecri, the brilliant toymaker, and his assistants are always creating new toys and gadgets for the younger and older children of the Kingdom of Light. The children especially love spending their time at his shop picking out their favorite ones. Many times the children give Hecri ideas about the toys and gadgets and together they create a fantastic toy or gadget that all the children want to play with.

Karen stopped talking to allow the Brian to continue when Corina curiously asked, "Do they have to pay for their toys?" All the grandchildren looked at Karen and Brian wondering about the same thing.

"No, no one has to pay for anything. All that is there is for everyone to enjoy and share," Karen answered smiling.

"Wow!!" the grandchildren said at the same time. "I would love to live there," Nigel said and everyone, even Jo and Lee, agreed, "Me, too."

The Mountaintop

KAREN AND BRIAN NOW had to tell their grand-children about the mission of the Light Beings and Brian began the story with the first mountaintop lesson.

As the Prince and the Princess grew older, the King and Queen wanted to show their children what the eagles could see from high in the sky. So, one day, with a wave of their hands, the Royal Family magically found themselves atop the highest mountain. They were so high up that the clouds were below them. The King waved his hand and the small fluffy clouds moved aside so they could see the kingdom below.

"Wow" exclaimed the Prince. PK whispered, "It's so big."

The King laughed, "Yes, Little One," he said softly, "this kingdom is so big that you cannot see where it begins and where it ends. All that is here is yours."

The Queen lovingly said to her children, "All that you want to do and all that you want to be, you will learn from us. Today, you will learn that everyone here has a mission, and today begins your preparation to accomplish the same mission."

The King then pointed to an area at a far distance and said, "Look, over there is a smaller kingdom. Our mission is to help the beings who live in that kingdom."

As the children looked to the area where the King pointed, they noticed that the area didn't have the glow of different colors and lights. There was still a glow around the area, but not of the same brightness and only with a few different colors, not like the thousands of colors and lights that surrounded their magical kingdom.

"It's not as bright as this place," the young Prince observed. The Princess nodded in agreement.

"That is because that kingdom contains both the Light and its opposite, the Shadow. It is called the Kingdom of Opposites," the King explained.

"What is it like there?" asked the Prince. The King and Queen settled into the chairs that magically appeared and signaled their children to do the same. Then the King and Queen began to tell them about the Kingdom of Opposites.

The King explained, "All that is here is also there. The birds that sing, the music from the trees, the flowers, the mountains, the oceans, and the animals that play together are also there. It is the same sky, the same sun, moon, and stars. There is also the same Light everywhere and in everything, but the Light is not as brilliant because over in that place the Shadow also exists. For the Light to come forth and shine through, the beings living there must remember that their Light is within and connect to it. This connection to their Light makes the Shadow disappear.

When this happens, the beings will then hear the music, see the beauty, and find joy, love, and peace because they have connected to us and to our kingdom. Their Light within will expand outward and touch everyone around them so they may also connect to their own inner Light, and their Light will also expand outward and that is the mission, to be the Light in that kingdom.

Our mission here is to help them so that the smaller kingdom can dispel the Shadow and become just like this kingdom, and together we become one Kingdom of Light."

The Queen continued, "But some beings have forgotten their mission and have forgotten that they have this magical Light within, and they end up attracting only the Shadow into their lives. There is no magic in the Shadow, there is only fear, and they do not hear the music or see the beauty; they live with so much pain and suffering and they end up destroying themselves, each other, and their beautiful kingdom.

The royal children gasped at these words.

"You mean even the trees and the flowers?" asked the Princess. "The animals and the oceans too?" asked the Prince.

"Sadly so," answered the Queen.

The young Prince, very confused with this explanation, asked, "Who lives there?"

The Queen smiled as she gently explained, "The beings who live there come from here. They are Light Beings just like you and everyone here. They have made the courageous choice to make the journey to enter and live in that kingdom to vanquish the shadows. So everyone who enters that place has the same mission, to be the Light and to remember that they are Light Beings and not beings of Shadow."

The Prince asked, "The beings who live there came from our kingdom?"

The King and Queen smiled at the incredulous look on their son's face.

The King explained, "Every being in that kingdom was shown what life would be like living in both Light and Shadow. They knew beforehand that it would not be easy living there, but they still chose to make the journey anyway. Those Light Beings are courageous. To help with their mission, they are each given unique gifts and talents to bring into that kingdom and share with the other beings there. The gifts and talents help make that place brighter, and when they share their gifts and talents with the other beings, it touches their Light within and they remember that they too have the same mission."

The King and Queen continue to explain that those beings in the smaller kingdom were well prepared for their journey. Each one chose how they would accomplish their mission through the use of their gifts and talents. They were shown by the Talent Experts in the magical kingdom how to perfect these talents, and these Experts have agreed that when the time is right to use these talents, they will help them from this side.

"All ideas, all creation, all solutions, all answers to questions come from here and make their way into that kingdom.

This is how the beings from both kingdoms fulfill the mission." the King and Queen continued.

The King then instructed his children to take a closer look at the other kingdom.

The children again noticed that the place was not as bright, but as they looked closer they did notice that there were some areas that were brighter than others.

Both children exclaimed excitedly, "Look, there are more lights on that side!"

The King and Queen both laughed at their excitement. They wanted their children to see how the mission was being accomplished.

They were told that the places that had more lights were the places where the beings remembered who they were, and every single time a being in that kingdom remembered who they were, they were instantly connected to this place of joy and their joy expanded outward touching all those around them and the shadows disappeared. The brighter areas were also places where help was being given and received. The King and Queen became quiet for a while so that their children could fully understand what was being explained to them.

The young Prince asked, "Which beings choose to go there?"

"Whoever wants to make the journey," answered the Queen smiling.

"How can I help them?" asked the young Prince. The Princess also nodded wondering how she could help too.

"When the time is right, you will choose the talents you wish to use and we will give the gifts to help you with your chosen talents. *You will learn from the Talent Experts here and you will also learn from the Learning Masters at the School of Learning. Did you know that you have already been helping with the mission?"* the King asked.

"We have?" both children asked at the same time. Both the King and Queen laughed. *"Whenever you told Mari from the Sweets Shoppe or Hecri from the Toy and Gadget Shoppe what you enjoyed from their shops, those ideas were sent to the smaller kingdom so the beings there could also enjoy them,"* the Queen informed her children. The children looked pleased at their contribution to the mission.

They ended their time at the mountaintop and the King placed his hands on the top of his children's heads to keep in what they learned on their first lesson. With a wave of his hand, the Royal family found themselves back on the ground. The King and Queen sent their children off to play with their friends. The brother and sister had a lot to think about that day. They now knew they had a mission to help those beings in the other kingdom who had forgotten why they were there.

Brian paused to let Karen continue.

"Oh, bummer, they have to go to school," Shane said.

"Yeah, but they already have a job waiting for them when they finish," Kay said enthusiastically.

In his usual jovial way, Shane immediately responded, "To vanquish shadows, that's the job. Oh, I forgot, you're going to be lawyer, that's the same thing. You vanquish your retainer's fee from your clients." Everyone laughed.

The Royal Court

AFTER THE LAUGHTER AND the teasing died down, Karen continued with the tale.

The Royal Court is made up of special Light Beings who serve the King and Queen. They have been given special talents to do a special job. These Beings are the Angees, the Talent Experts, and the Learning Masters.

The Angees are the largest group in the Royal Court. There are millions of Angees who serve the Royal Family. The group called the Protectors stand over 10 feet tall and they are made up of white lights. They surround and protect the Kingdom of Light and they know who leaves or enters the Kingdom.

Then there are the Angees known as the Messengers. The Messengers carry messages from the King to those in the smaller kingdom. The King is always happy to help those in the smaller kingdom carry out their mission. The King always knows when his help is needed because those Light Beings use their magical Light to connect to the King's Light. He happily sends the Messenger Angees to the smaller kingdom to give the help that is needed. Sometimes the help they need may be an answer to a question, a solution to a problem, or an idea to make life better in the smaller kingdom.

The Messengers move with lightning speed from the Kingdom of Light to the Kingdom of Opposites to deliver the King's messages. They move so fast that it seems like they are flying. You know when the Messengers are going by because you see tiny sparks of silver and blue from their Light and you can feel the breeze on your face. When they arrive in the smaller kingdom, they whisper the message into the ear of the one needing help and stay with that being to continue to help them and their Light surrounds and protects them.

Some of the lighted areas that the Royal children saw are the Messenger Angees who have been sent to help those needing the King's help.

There is another group of Angees called the Guardians. The King gives instructions to each Guardian Angee who is sent to accompany each being in the smaller kingdom. The King tells them, "Guard them and protect them from harm, gently remind them of who they are, but do not interfere with the choices they make. They have the free will to do and act as they please. You can lovingly and gently remind them that they are Beings of Light but each being must make the choice of the Light or the Shadow."

Whenever someone makes the choice of being in the Shadow, their Guardian whispers softly, "You are a Being of Light. Be the Light." Whenever someone makes the choice of being in the Light, their Guardian applauds their choice and the light around them gets brighter making the person feel good about the decision they made and allowing them to feel the King's and Queen's smiles upon them. These are more of the lighted areas that the children saw coming from this kingdom.

There are also Guardian Angees assigned to guard the other living things in the smaller kingdom. There are Guardians for all the animals including the birds and the fish. There are also Guardians for the trees, flowers, and the mountains, for these are also living creations. If you look really closely, you'll know they are there because there is a soft glow around them. This glow is coming from the lights of the Guardians.

The next largest group in the Royal Court is the Talent Experts. These are beings who are experts in a special talent and they teach other beings how to be creative with the same talents. These talents may be in music, art, medicine, science, business, inventions, writing, speaking, entertaining, teaching, and so much more. They help prepare those beings who will be going into the smaller kingdom as well as the beings who have chosen to stay and help from this side. Those who remain are always ready to assist when they are asked for help from those in the smaller kingdom. They give the ideas or solutions needed to better express their talents in unique, creative ways and the Messenger Angees deliver the message.

The other group in the Royal Court is called the Learning Masters. These are the Teachers. They are found in the

Learning Centers in the Kingdom of Light. In these Learning Centers, all Light Beings are shown many scenes that are occurring in the smaller kingdom that happen in the battle between the Light and the Shadow. It is after viewing these scenes at the Learning Centers that Light Beings choose how their gifts and talents will help vanquish the Shadow in the smaller kingdom. It is also from here that some beings decide to make the journey and live in the smaller kingdom. Many beings who enter the smaller kingdom seem to think that they have been in that place before, but they are remembering the scenes they saw in the Learning Center.

Karen stopped talking and the grandchildren waited for her to continue. "Let's take a break, kids, like an intermission, because we are moving this party outside so we can be under the stars. Grab your popcorn, your drink, your jacket, and a blanket and follow us outside." The grandchildren obediently stood up, took their things, and followed Karen and Brian outside.

They marched out onto the sand and Brian gave each grandchild instructions on where to spread out their blanket. Soon they were all lying side by side as they looked up into the night sky. It was a beautiful autumn night, that was not chilly, the moon barely visible behind a cloud and the sky filled with stars.

"Look at all those stars," Jo said softly. "Grandpa, is that the Kingdom of Light up there?"

"It might be somewhere in there among the stars, but the lights from the Kingdom of Light are much brighter than the stars we see here. The night sky in the Kingdom of Light has stars that are so bright that they seem close enough that you can almost touch them."

Everyone was quiet for a few minutes, each grandchild in their private thoughts as they tried to picture what that night sky would look like.

Karen said, "There is a myth that was told by the ancient people when they were looking up at the sky, just like we are now, and they wondered the same thing. They said that the sky is like this huge ceiling and beyond the ceiling are lights and there are these little holes in this ceiling and the stars that we see are the lights coming through those tiny holes." All the grandchildren thought about this for a while, picturing the many holes in the ceiling as they tried to count the stars of the night.

⤙ The Rainbow ⤚

BRIAN CONTINUED THE STORY as they all gazed at the stars.

The Prince and PK are happy children and all the children in this kingdom are happy children and they enjoy playing with each other. PK and her friends especially enjoy playing in the field of flowers. They run through the fields, pick the glowing flowers, and they put them in their hair. Their laughter can be heard as they run and play and chase the colorful glowing butterflies that always join them in the fields.

One beautiful sunny day, PK and her two favorite friends, Shajula and Brilola, were playing in the field. Brilola picked the different flowers and with the ribbons she brought with her, she made three little crowns. PK and Shajula squealed with delight as Brilola handed them their crowns to wear. Shajula loved to dance and she was always showing the girls a new dance. They danced and laughed as they saw their own lights twirling around them as they spun. Then it began to rain lightly. The girls continued their laughing and dancing for they knew that the light rain would stop soon.

The girls suddenly stopped laughing when they noticed that the King and Queen were standing there smiling and watching them. With a wave of the King's hand, the rain immediately stopped and the sun peeked out from behind the rain cloud above. Smiling at the girls with their flower and ribbon crowns, the Queen called the children to gather around. The children did so for they knew that whenever the Royal Rulers showed up, something wonderful was about to be revealed.

The King pointed to the flowers with the raindrops still on their petals and said to the girls, "Listen to their music. They are singing their praises to the sun and the rain." The girls listened and shrieked in delight as they heard the music of the flowers. Each flower had its own special music and together they sounded like a beautiful orchestra. The girls looked around them in this field of colorful flowers and noticed that as each group of flowers vibrated their own music, their colors twinkled like colorful stars. It was the most beautiful sight that the young girls had seen and they all clapped and whispered softly, "Wow!"

The Queen then said, "Each petal opens in song as it faces upward to both the rain and sun and they twinkle as if they are winking and saying 'thank you' for the warmth and the rain. Each flower also gives thanks to the ground where they get their food and they say 'thank you' by singing their praises and growing and spreading and becoming fields of beauty to blanket the ground in love. Not only does each flower have its own music, but it also has its own special fragrance that gets released into the air whenever it dances with the gentle breezes that come to visit the flowers in the fields."

Just then, a gentle breeze came by and sure enough, the nearby flowers began to sway as if they were dancing with the breeze. The girls could smell the sweet fragrance from the flowers and giggled and clapped again.

The King then began to speak, and as he spoke, his voice could be heard throughout the Kingdom. "Everything that is created is created to help everything else grow and become the best that it can be." His voice boomed throughout the Kingdom. The Prince and his friends were swimming and playing at the beach and they stopped talking so they could hear what the King was saying. The children and everyone in the Kingdom knew that if the King or the Queen's voice could be heard from wherever they were, something important was being said and should be heard. Everyone stopped what they were doing to listen to the words of their powerful and wise King.

Likewise, those in the smaller kingdom could also hear the King's important words, but the words came like a whisper in the wind. Those who were surrounded by the Light could hear the King very clearly, but those who were surrounded by the Shadow could not hear the words.

The King continued his lesson for all to hear. "Above you in the sky are the sun and the clouds. The sun gives light and keeps us warm. The clouds carry the rain and they float all over looking out for the flowers and the trees that need the rain. They listen to the music that drifts upward to them and when they know that part of the kingdom needs the rain, the clouds happily open up and let the rain fall downward while the other clouds move toward the sun and cleverly cover up the heat from the sun until enough rain is released. Once the clouds scatter the raindrops below, the other clouds move away from the face of the sun and they continue on their merry way floating above. Remember that everything begins again to create again. Once the rain gives what the ground, the lakes, and the oceans need, the raindrops return again to the clouds. Just as the blooms open in their full beauty and release their own unique fragrance, they fall to the ground, and new flowers or trees come forth and the process begins again. Nothing, absolutely nothing created ever stops creating."

The Queen continued and her gentle voice could be heard everywhere. "Learning is also the same process. All that a being learns passes on to more beings and the process begins again and again. It is all about creating and growing with each other to help each other. This is the secret of a happy life. To grow and help others to grow."

The King and Queen reached out to take some of the flowers that the young girls had picked and as they held these twinkling colorful flowers, the King said, "Behold, the flowers have sung and danced and now they will share their beauty in the sky."

As the King and Queen threw the flowers upward, the most spectacular thing happened. Hundreds of colorful arches appeared all over the place. The colorful flowers became colorful arches. Each arch rose from the ground up to the sky for miles and then it arched back down to the ground. One after another after another and on and on the arches of many colors filled the sky. It was so magnificent and spectacular that everyone in the Kingdom of Light could see the arches for miles and miles.

At the same time, these colorful arches also appeared in the Kingdom of Opposites. Only one or two could be seen and only in areas where there was more Light than Shadow. Instead of the many colors that were seen in the Kingdom of Light, only seven of these colors were seen in the Kingdom of Opposites. These colorful arches were called "rainbows" and were seen in both kingdoms when the rain and the sun had completed their dance. Before the King and Queen left the field of flowers now filled with many arches, they placed their hands on the tops of the girls' heads so they would always remember the lesson about the dance of creation and the sharing with each one to grow and create again and again.

Brian stopped talking and Corina softly said, "Grandpa, I sometimes hear music and I think it's coming from the trees or the flowers outside. Is it coming from the trees and the flowers?" Her grandfather lovingly answered, "If you listen very closely, you can still hear their music."

Little Jo said, "I think I sometimes hear it too."

"Me, too," Lee said and soon the rest of the group started to nod in agreement as if they also remembered hearing music coming from trees or the flowers at some time.

Nigel then said, "If the smaller kingdom could only see seven of the colors of the rainbow, how many colors do you think the original rainbow had?"

His grandmother easily answered his curious question, "The original rainbow had three times the color, so there were 21 different colors. Could you just imagine how magnificent that looked?"

"Yeah!!" came a unison response. Each grandchild became silent as they each visualized what a rainbow of 21 colors would look like.

The Sunflowers

AFTER THE KIDS SHARED their thoughts on the dance, the music, and the hundreds of arches, Karen continued with the story.

One morning, the Queen took the Princess for a walk. PK loved her special time with her mother. This was her learning time with her and it was also the time when PK asked her questions and her mother laughed at some of them but she always answered them.

They walked through the field of flowers and came upon an opening and the Queen said, "Here is an empty patch of ground and here you will create whatever you want to grow. Look around you at the trees, the flowers, the grasses, the mountains, the sky, the clouds and see how they all fit in with each other, living together in this space and helping each other to grow." PK remembered the lesson given when the rainbows were created.

The Queen continued, "Today, I will teach you to use the power of your Light to create whatever you wish to see grow in this empty patch of ground. Your creation will add to the beauty that already exists and it will be your contribution to all that is."

"How do I create?" asked the young Princess.

"Use your imagination," answered the Queen as she smiled at her daughter. Before her daughter could ask "What's an imagination?" the Queen began explaining. "An imagination is what you create in your mind first before you see it appear and it can be anything you want it to be."

"Anything?" asked PK.

"Anything," replied the Queen.

The Princess looked around her as she saw the beauty and the glowing color around everything. "It is all so beautiful already, what could I create to make it more beautiful?" she thought. Then she looked up at the sky and saw the sun giving light to all.

She remembered the lesson of the dance of the rain and the sun and the rainbows that were created from that dance. She then looked at the field of flowers in the distance and then an idea came to her. She also suddenly remembered the King telling her and Gi that all ideas first come from this place and were then given to the beings in the smaller kingdom.

She got excited and she turned to her mother and asked excitedly, "I have an idea, is this my imagination?"

"Yes it is," smiled the Queen. Her young daughter understood the power of creation. "Now, in order for your idea to become real, you must speak it and believe it and your special magical light will let it happen. Your special magical light is connected with the Creative Light that creates everything we see around us. Therefore when you speak your idea, it becomes the power that activates that Creative Light and your idea takes form, and before you know it, it shows up, just like magic!"

The Princess smiled at her mother; she just knew that the Queen would love her idea too. "Well," she began, "I would like to bring the sun down here and let it come up from the ground so it could smile at the sun up there," as she pointed to the sky. "I want to create a flower just like the sun!"

"Tell me more about this sunflower," the Queen urged her daughter and PK got more and more excited and said "That's it, Mother, we'll call it the Sunflower! And it won't be just one flower; let's create thousands and thousands of sunflowers, a whole field of sunflowers. The sunflowers will look up at the sun when it rises in the morning and flowers will move as they follow the sun across the sky."

"What will the flowers do when the sun sets on the other side? Will they close up and open again when the sun rises in the morning?" asked the Queen.

"Oh no, they will stay open all night and wait to greet the sun the next morning. That way, the sun will always be here with us." PK answered.

The Queen smiled proudly at her daughter's beautiful idea of keeping the sun at night.

"Open your hands," the Queen instructed her daughter, and as PK opened up her tiny hands, the Queen placed some small seeds in them. "Now, close your eyes," the Queen again instructed her daughter, "and see this field of sunflowers in your imagination and see how it looks, imagine how the stems, the petals and the leaves will look, how tall or how small they will grow and how many flowers will be on each stem. Once you see them clearly in your imagination, believe that you will see them grow just as you are seeing them in your imagination now."

The Princess did as she was told and saw clearly how her sunflowers would look. They would be yellow and would glow a golden color. With her eyes closed, PK didn't see that as she was imagining her field of sunflowers her light grew brighter and the seeds in her hands began to glow.

The Queen knew at that moment that her young daughter truly believed in her magical power to create whatever she desired.

PK opened her eyes, looked up at her mother and said very softly, "I saw them, Mother, thousands and thousands of sunflowers, and you can see them from far away and they look so pretty."

The Queen smiled at her daughter and watched as PK gently and lovingly sprinkled the seeds on the ground. As they walked away hand in hand the Queen explained to the young Princess that she must now wait for the seed to sprout her flowers, and she explained once again the dance that must happen between the soil, the sun, and the rain.

For several days, PK watched as her field of sunflowers grew and grew until finally the flowers opened up wide and smiled at the sun in the sky. Just as she had imagined there were thousands and thousands of sunflowers, each with glowing orange and yellow petals just like the rays of the sun. She was right; she could see this field of brightly glowing tiny suns for miles all around.

PK didn't know then that right at that same moment there were also thousands of sunflowers that sprouted in open fields in the Kingdom of Opposites. Those living in the smaller kingdom were excited and happy when they saw the fields covered with beautiful sunflowers. Many did not understand where or how the flowers showed up, but some did understand that something as beautiful as these flowers showing up could only mean that it came from the magic of the Kingdom of Light.

That evening, the King and Queen walked through PK's field of sunflowers as they discussed her creation. They were proud of their young daughter's achievement and her connection to her magical creative powers.

Karen then paused and allowed the kids to talk about what they had just heard. Some loved that PK chose to create the sunflowers, while others, especially the grandsons, talked about what they would grow if they were given magic seeds. There was more laughter and more teasing among the group. Brian and Karen looked at each other and smiled. Their grandchildren were using their imaginations on what they would create in their patch of ground.

⏀ Sergie ⏀

BRIAN QUIETED DOWN THE group and continued with the story.

One day the Prince and his friends, Trevori and Joni were playing at the beach. Joni brought a football and the three boys were throwing the football to each other while riding on the backs of the dolphins. Trevori was always clowning around with his friends and they were always laughing and having a good time.

The Prince threw the football to Joni and as he and his dolphin raced to catch the ball, Trevori would show up, as if from nowhere and have his dolphin splash the water so hard that Joni couldn't see the ball. Joni missed the pass and they all started laughing again.

The King was watching them from atop a small hill not far from the ocean. He saw that the young Prince especially enjoyed swimming with the dolphins and riding on their backs going up and down in the water. The King stepped forward so the children could see that he was there. He called them to the shore and as they gathered around him, they knew that they were about to hear something of great importance.

As the King spoke, his voice could be heard all over the Kingdom, just as it could when he was in the field of flowers with PK and her friends. He explained that there was a whole world of marine life that lived in the oceans. They came in all sizes and all kinds, from the plant life to the coral, and from the smallest fish to the largest of all. They all got along and had plenty of food to eat and they played and swam alongside each other. They each had their own song and together they sang a symphony that could be heard only in the water.

"Listen closely," he instructed the boys. As they did, they could hear the music coming from the water. With a wave of his hand, the whales came up from the deep. There were hundreds of them gathered together at the command of the King and they began singing. It was the most beautiful music the children ever heard. It was a beautiful sight to behold. When their music was done, they bowed to the King and returned to the deep.

All the young Prince and his friends could say was "Wow!" Everyone in the Kingdom also heard the songs of the whales and they had stopped whatever they were doing to enjoy the spectacular music.

Then the dolphins, hundreds of them, also jumped up from the water and they seem to applaud the concert of the whales as their fins clapped together. Then they did their little dance on the water and sang their own music and leaped, twirled, and dove. The King and the children laughed, delighted at their performance.

The King turned to his son and said, "Which one is your favorite?" The young prince pointed to his dolphin, and the King said, "Call him to you."

"How do I do that?" asked Gi. "I usually just swim to him."

"You have dominion over the lives that live in the oceans," he said, and again his voice carried to every corner of the kingdom so all could hear. "Protect them and see that no harm comes to them. They will not come unto the land to harm you. Those on the land and those in the water together exist in harmony with each other and share the fruits of the Kingdom. The ocean sparkles like diamonds as their waves dance with the sun, the rain, and the wind. The marine life within these waters keeps the oceans in place. Each in their own place and each in harmony with each other."

Once again, the King gently said to his son, "Call your favorite to you; use your magical power, and he will come at your command." The Prince did as he was told and as he called his favorite swimming companion to him, his lights sparkled and grew and his lights expanded to reach the dolphin. And both lights, his and dolphin's, merged into one brilliant light, and the dolphin made his way to the young Prince.

Gi and his friends watched in awe as the dolphin swam toward them and waited on the edge of the shore.

"This one shall be your pet. You will listen to his song and know that there is a language being spoken and you will learn that language and you will speak with each other and he will teach you about his life. From there, you will learn how to protect and keep him and all that live in this water world from outside harm," the King instructed his young son.

Prince Gi nodded his head; he understood what his father had said. The young Prince was given his first training for his mission. "Now," said the King as he smiled at the Prince, "what shall you name your friend?"

The Prince already knew that answer, for he had already named his friend, the day they met. "Father, his name is Sergie," answered the Prince proudly.

"Sergie, it shall be," responded the King. Sergie heard his name and started clapping his fins and began singing and dancing again. The King and the children laughed.

The King then turned to the two friends who had witnessed the event and said "You, too, can do the same." Knowing that his son would teach the others how to expand their magical light to call their own dolphins to them, the King turned to walk away.

But, before he did, he did what he always did whenever a lesson was imparted to his son. He placed his hand on top of his head sending this knowledge through him, so he would never forget what he learned that day.

The boys took off with their dolphins and from that moment on the language between them and the dolphins became clear. The King smiled proudly for right at that very moment the beings at the smaller kingdom could hear the songs of the whales and the language of the dolphins.

Brian stopped talking and the group started talking all at once. "Wow!" Nigel exclaimed, "That is so cool." He then stood up and mimicked the scene, "I command you, Sergie, swim to me." Everyone laughed and everyone also stood up and mimicked the scene in their own individual way. Lee and Jo even got into the fun.

Once the group settled back on their blankets, Karen continued with the story.

On one of their daily mountaintop lessons, which the Royal Family looked forward to, the King and Queen prepared their children for their important mission to help those in the smaller kingdom.

The King and Queen talked about talents. "A talent is a special gift and no two talents are alike," the Queen informed them. "Every being is given more than one talent that holds its own unique light that needs to shine. These talents are our gifts to you and they are to be shared with others. Remember this always," she instructed them.

"You get to choose your talents," the King continued. "It is these talents that will help you in your mission to help save the smaller kingdom."

They then pointed out the talents of the toymaker, the scientists, the baker, the teachers, and others. The children understood about sharing and teaching others to develop their talents with the power of their magical light that is within.

The children were reminded of how PK used her talent to create her sunflowers for all to enjoy and that they needed to remember to be thankful to the sun above. They were also reminded of how Gi had used his talent to communicate with the dolphins and teach his friends how to understand their language. Those were just some examples of the talents that they would use to help those who needed the help.

The Queen further explained, "All our gifts are already within you, within your lights, and as you grow, one by one they will reveal themselves to you and you will seek those who are Experts of the same talent here and they will lovingly show you how to also become Experts and master your unique talents."

The children talked excitedly about what other talents they would like to have. The young Prince talked about how much he was learning from his pet dolphin, Sergie, and the lives of those that lived in the ocean. He pointed out that he was enjoying the music of the whales and he found himself singing with them. Gi then announced to all of them, "I shall learn more about music from the Music Experts here."

PK talked about her field of sunflowers and her enjoyment of the colors of the flowers and she also proudly announced, "I shall learn more about flowers and colors, for they are so beautiful and they make everything around them even more beautiful."

The King and Queen smiled proudly at their children. They were still growing and learning and they would choose other talents and master them for their mission.

When they left their mountaintop, the children eagerly ran off to get lessons from the different Talent Experts. Gi went off to find the Music Experts and PK went off to find the Art Experts to learn about colors.

❧ Wings ❧

A T THIS POINT IN the story, Brian interrupted
Karen and with his eyes twinkling, he said to his
cousin, "Let me tell this part." Karen smiled and nodded and Brian continued.

PK had been enjoying her time and learning so much
with the Art Experts in the kingdom and she was given a
large palette filled with many colors with which to prac-
tice her artwork. She was so delighted at how the colors of
her artwork glowed and twinkled. She giggled every time
she mixed two or more colors together and came up with a
totally different color.

One day when she and her friends were running and
playing in the field of flowers, she dipped her paintbrush into
the colors of her palette and started running through the field,
dropping paint on the petals of the flowers. She and her friends
laughed when they saw how pretty the little drops of blue paint
were on a yellow flower or the little pink color on the white
flowers. Then they heard the flowers singing, their music letting
her know that she had just added more beauty to their petals.

She gave each friend a paintbrush and they all ran through the fields dripping tiny drops of paint on the petals. Brilola caught a butterfly and she began painting new colors on it. Shajula and PK did the same thing.

She didn't know that the King and Queen were watching from a distance, pleased at their daughter's discovery of artistic talent. She also didn't know that right at that moment more and more of these multicolored flowers and butterflies were showing up in the smaller kingdom, much to the delight of the beings there.

Pleased with her use of her artistic talents and ready to give their daughter her very own pet, the King and Queen presented their young daughter with a gift. It was a beautiful white horse that could fly.

The Royal Family gathered together on that special occasion and PK hugged each one when she saw the magnificent horse that was all hers. She instantly called him Wings and they all laughed. Gi was very happy that his sister had Wings and he had Sergie. They both knew their responsibility to care for and love their pets.

PK spent many hours riding on the ground and soaring up and flying. The townspeople smiled whenever they saw this white horse flying by with his wings spread out wide and PK on his back with her twinkling colors swirling all around her like a light show for all to see.

One day as PK was walking through her field of sunflowers that always reminded her of the all that the sun did to help everything on the ground grow and bloom, she remembered that magical day in the field of flowers—that day when the King threw up a bunch of flowers and created the arches of colors called rainbows. A thanksgiving to the dance of the sun and the rain, he told them that day.

PK suddenly had an idea. She looked up at the beautiful silver and blue sky and the golden sun just going over the mountains. PK took her palette of colors and a large paintbrush and mounted Wings. "Take me to sky!" she instructed her beautiful horse. Wings spread his wings and together they soared higher than he had ever taken her. With her large brush dripping with reds, oranges, golds, and pinks, PK spread the colors across the sky. The streaks of gold, yellow, red, and pink lit the silver and blue sky. On and on she painted the streaks as Wings flew her one way and then another. Some of the clouds moved aside and some of the clouds stayed where they were and were also painted. Some of the paint dripped onto the trees below, making the green leaves turn yellow, orange, and red.

The beings in the kingdom below looked up and stared in awe at the beautiful painting they were looking at. The King, Queen, and Gi laughed at PK having fun with the largest canvas ever—the whole sky.

At the same time, the beings in the smaller kingdom also saw their sky fill with streaks of yellow, red, orange, and pink as the sun was going below the horizon. They also saw that many trees had leaves of yellow, red, and orange. No one knew what had happened. The experts who were studying the things in the sky, such as the sun, moon, stars, and clouds, were seen running around looking through all their equipment to find out what those colors meant and where they came from. Their equipment could not see that PK from the Kingdom of Light was painting the sky for all to enjoy. Some of the beings were seen running and hiding thinking that the sky was going to fall upon them while those connected to their lights knew that somehow it was the magic being shared from beyond.

After PK was done with her magnificent artwork, she joined her family and the Art Experts below. She was congratulated on the discovery and use of her artistic gift. The Queen, smiling at her young daughter, said, "What shall you call your painting?"

"That's easy," replied PK, "it is called 'colors of the sun' because now the sunflowers are up in the sky saying thank you to the sun." They were all pleased with the name she gave her artwork.

The King said, "How about instead of your sunflowers just saying thank you, your sunflowers also say 'goodnight' to the sun? Each time the sun starts to go over the mountaintop, your painting will appear again saying its goodnight."

"Yes, oh yes. Thank you, Father," the excited young Princess said jumping up and down and clapping her hands as her own colors twinkled and twinkled, making everyone around her laugh again. PK's "colors of the sun" artwork stayed in the sky until the night sky covered it with the stars and the moon. The next day and every day after that, the artwork appeared again saying "goodnight" to the sun and hello to the moon and the millions of stars that light up the night sky.

To the amazement of the beings in the smaller kingdom, they witnessed the same event every day just before nightfall. The scientists explained this colorful event as being from the rays of the setting sun. Soon both kingdoms came to know the artwork as simply, "the sunset." The scientists gave up trying to figure out how the colorful rays suddenly appeared and how many trees now have leaves of the same color as the painting in the sky. After a while, everyone just enjoyed their colorful gifts from beyond.

Brian ended his part of the story, pleased that he had presented it well as Karen gave him a nod of approval and waited for the group to jump in with their comments.

The grandchildren were talking all at once. "What a place to live!", "Swimming with the dolphins, flying on a horse!"

Then the group quieted down and was told it was time they got back into the house. As they gathered their things and walked to the house, they talked about the sunset painting. They knew that every time they saw a sunset, they would think of PK on her flying horse painting the sky for all to see.

When they got back into the house, each grandchild took his or her place in the living room, getting comfortable and waiting for the story to continue. Karen looked at them and said, "Oh, you still want to hear more?"

"Yes! Don't stop now. What else happens?" came the responses from all.

Brian and Karen both laughed at their enthusiasm and settled into their storytelling chairs to continue where they left off.

A Trip to the
Kingdom of Opposites

KAREN PICKED UP THE story at this point and
continued.

*The Royal children are now grown up, and in one of their
daily lessons on the mountaintop, they are taught how the
Light is more powerful than the Shadow and how important
it is that everyone in both kingdoms completes their mission.*

*"Until they do," the King explained one day, "they will
continue to live in the world of shadows. Once each mission
is complete, the beings will return back here, for this is their
home, their kingdom."*

*The Queen gently explained further, "To live in that smaller
kingdom is not an easy path; that is why each being must be
prepared to learn to live with both the Light and the Shadow."*

*The Prince looked very serious as he announced, "I
want to make the journey. I want to be the Light for that
kingdom. I want to bring joy through music and knowledge
about the marine life. I don't want to just learn here and
send ideas to them through the Messenger Angees, I want to
go there and show them and remind them."*

PK looked shocked at her brother's announcement. "No, Gi, you can't go. Stay here with me." Gi smiled at his beautiful sister. The King and Queen smiled at their son.

"If that is what you want to do, let us go there and see what life is like in the Kingdom of Opposites," the King responded.

"Go there now?" both children asked at the same time.

"Why not now? The King and I are always in both places at the same time. The only thing that separates the two kingdoms is a thin veil. The Light Beings who chose to make the journey pass through this veil and come out the other side as beings of the Kingdom of Opposites. But for this trip, we'll just go through the veil just as we are. We will be invisible to everyone there, but those who are connected to their Light will sense our presence," the Queen answered.

With a wave of the King's hand, the Royal Family found themselves atop another mountain. It looked like the same mountaintop where they took their daily lessons, but it wasn't.

"Where are we?" asked the Prince.

"We are in the Kingdom of Opposites. Look below; some things look the same and some do not," replied the King. As the children looked they saw the same hills, same sky, same clouds, and the same meadows, grasses, and trees that they saw from their own mountaintop in their kingdom, but somehow it just looked different here. They were not glowing with brilliant colors.

In the next moment, they found themselves standing on the ground below. "The light is not bright," observed the Princess. "There is no music anywhere," observed the Prince.

"There is always music coming from everything created, even here, but you have to listen very closely," answered the Queen. The children listened and soon they heard the familiar music from the grass, trees, and hills. They also noticed that just as the lights were not as bright, they could barely hear the music. They walked through the meadow and noticed cows grazing nearby. As they walked closer to them, the cows looked up as though they could see them.

"They sense our lights, but they cannot see us," the King said. They saw some farmhouses nearby and they saw children playing atop a small hill.

"Oh! They are picking flowers and chasing butterflies. Look, there are sunflowers here, too!" PK exclaimed.

The Royal Family also noticed the Angees that were standing by watching the children. "Those Angees are protecting them," the King informed his children. The Angees could see the Royal Family and waved at them and they waved back smiling.

The Royal children noticed that the children of the smaller kingdom looked different. They each had a small glow around them, but their lights did not spread out or twinkle like their own. They seemed to have a covering over them. The Queen answered their unspoken question. "That's their body. Every being who comes into this Kingdom wears a body like that. Although they look different from you, they are still the same

Light Beings underneath that body and they still possess the magical powers of their own lights. Every being wears a body when they come here for their mission and they leave the body behind when they return home."

Just then, one of the girls chasing a butterfly stumbled over a small rock and began falling over the edge of the small hill. Right at that moment her Guardian Angee reached over and caught her and made her land safely on the ground. The little girl looked up at the Angee as if she could see her and smiled as she ran back up the hill to join the others.

The King and Queen explained that the young children do see that a Guardian Angee is always with them. "Each being who enters this kingdom begins as a baby and grows up.

"While they are young, they can still feel the joy that comes from the Light within. They see everything for the first time through their eyes. They play, they laugh, and they spread the joy that comes from their Light within their small body. Everyone around them smiles as they feel their Light and delight in all that they are seeing.

"As they get older, they have opposite feelings of joy because they now notice the shadows more than the Light. They soon begin to forget about their Guardian Angee who is always with them," the Queen gently explained to her children.

"Joy is the one feeling that will always connect you to who you truly are, a Light Being from the Kingdom of Light," the King explained. Once again, he placed his hand over their heads so they would always remember this lesson on joy.

With another wave of his hand, the King took his family to another part of the town. This time they found themselves in the downtown area where the people there were rushing to work.

"Oh!" gasped PK and Gi. "What is that? That is not music," exclaimed the Prince.

"That is what they call noise," answered the Queen gently as she watched the surprised looks on her children's faces. They were watching the rush hour traffic. Car horns were blaring, people were yelling at each other. People were just rushing to get to where they needed to be at this time of the day. People crossing the streets were not smiling. They were frowning and looking at their watches. There were Guardian Angees here too. They watched as a Guardian Angee stopped a being from being hit by a car that was going by.

"There is more Shadow here because the beings here are not feeling joy. Because they are surrounded by the Shadow, they are feeling all that is opposite of joy, love, peace, and being happy. They have forgotten how to make the Shadow disappear. Look closely and find those who have their inner lights turned on," instructed the King.

As the children looked closely, they could see that some of the beings had their inner lights turned on very brightly and some had inner lights that were not as bright. They saw a being help another being cross the street. They watched as the lights of the one helping got brighter and magically extended outward to touch the other. As this happened, the light of other being began to shine from within, until both lights expanded wider and wider as they smiled at each other. They also noticed that their expanded lights seem to touch the others around them and soon these beings' inner lights also shone through. They all seemed to be smiling at what was going on.

"That is an example of an act of kindness. As both lights are expanded outward, they touch the inner Light of all those who are observing this act of kindness," the Queen gently explained.

The King continued, "The joy that comes from even one act of kindness will remove the Shadow instantly."

The children were silent as they watched the shadows disappear around those watching the one act of kindness. They also noticed that the Angees were applauding. The Royal children were witnessing a magical light show.

The children watched in silence and thought of ways to help, to teach, and to share their talents to bring Light into this kingdom. Before they left, the saw other acts of kindness. Some were talking and laughing. Some were holding the doors open for others to enter a building as each being smiled at the other. Each time they saw an act of kindness, they also saw the beings' lights expand and the shadows around them disappear like magic and more Angees smiling and applauding.

They also noticed that the younger children seemed to look in their direction. They seemed to feel their presence and smile as if they knew a secret that the grownups did not know. Before the King waved his hand to return them to their own mountaintop, both the King and Queen placed their hands on the tops of their children's heads so they would always remember their lesson on kindness and joy.

When the Royal Family returned to their kingdom, the children were quiet. The King and Queen watched them.

PK finally said, "Wow! That was something. Gi, do you still want to live there?"

The Prince proudly said, "More than ever. I want to be the Light for that place and for all those who I will meet. Don't you want to go there, PK, and share all that you've learned with those who need our help?"

The Princess thought about her brother's question and quietly said, "I'm not sure yet."

The King and Queen both laughed and assured her, "You have time to change your mind, but remember that you will also be helping from this side and you can also help your brother while he is there. You can see him any time, you know. All you have to do is use your magic and you'll be there watching him and reminding him of this place, so he'll remember, should he forget that he is a Royal child and a Light Being."

The Prince announced, "I shall never forget who I am and why I am there."

The King and Queen happily smiled at their children as they ran off to expand their talents and they wondered if the Prince would forget once he got there.

More Talents Revealed

KAREN STOPPED SPEAKING AND the grandchildren were unusually quiet, thinking about what they just heard, and Brian continued.

After that first trip to the smaller kingdom, the Royal children talked about what they saw and what they wanted to change. The King and Queen continued to watch their children grow as their talents began to reveal themselves. The Prince was learning so much about those that live in the water with the help of his pet Sergie and from the Experts. He also learned that the beings in the smaller kingdom are given the knowledge to protect the lives that live in the deep. He watched as the Experts here gave messages to the Angees to deliver to the scientists there.

He was also spending more time with the Music Experts. He found that he could not only play the musical instruments there, but that he could sing and even write his own music. He sang with the whales and played the music of the deep and the music from the trees and the flowers.

PK was learning about the different types of plants and their purposes. Some plants bloomed with beautiful flowers and smelled good, and some plants bore fruits and leaves for eating. PK was also spending some of her time learning from the Medicine Experts about the different types of plants and how those plants could help the bodies of the beings in the smaller kingdom. Together the children shared what they have learned and talked about what they would do in their mission to the Kingdom of Opposites.

On one of their daily mountaintop lessons, the young Prince performed his musical talents for them. He had taken a couple of his favorites instruments and he played and then sang. It was beautiful and they applauded his new talent. The King especially loved music and he was so proud of his son. He then waved his hands as if he was making a command, and a choir Angees appeared and sang a beautiful song.

The music from the mountains and from the trees below played their music with the Angees. All could be heard from below and above and even beyond to the smaller kingdom. The magic from the music filled every place and the Light Beings all stopped what they were doing to listen. Some of the beings in the smaller kingdom also stopped to listen to this beautiful music that seemed to be coming from everywhere.

The musicians in the smaller kingdom stopped and became inspired by what they were hearing and started writing the notes. They didn't understand where it was coming from, but they stopped to listen, and they felt like they were going to explode with the feeling of joy. After the performance, everyone who heard the music clapped and clapped. It was truly magnificent!

"There is music in all things," the King explained. "Music touches the magical light that is in everyone and everything. When music reaches deep inside, the vibration from the music vibrates with everyone's special music, and they vibrate together creating a symphony that is the music of creation itself." He looked at his son and said. "Bring the music that is within you to all those who have forgotten their music and teach them the magic of their own music and it will bring them joy and help them remember who they truly are."

The Prince asked how the beings in the smaller kingdom could hear their own music when the place they saw was filled with noise.

"The music is within. The noise is outside. If you stop and listen to the music within, the noise on the outside fades away. Music is the Light and noise is the Shadow. The Shadow cannot exist if you turn on the Light that is within. Joy that is within is then released and it expands and expands touching all those around and the Shadow fades away. You saw how an act of kindness expands the Light from within. Sharing your talents for others to enjoy is another way to spread the Light. Helping and teaching each other is still another way. All it takes is one being, then another being, then another, until all their lights are on. Then, you have created a kingdom of Light. It's all about the magic within. The music of creation that you've just heard is my music.

When the noise seems to be loud, stop and take the time to go within and listen to my music, for you will always carry my music with you everywhere you go and in everything you do in this kingdom and in the other kingdom. Remember that always."

He then placed his hand atop both children so they would always remember this lesson in music and joy.

⌒ Lessons in Sharing ⌒

BOTH CHILDREN TALK ABOUT *what they have*
learned from the Talent Experts in the kingdom. PK
shared with Gi what the Medicine Experts had taught her
about the plants, flowers, and trees and all about the art and
colors she'd learned about from the Art Experts. Gi shared
what he had learned about the lives in the ocean and about
music and singing. The King and the Queen listened to their
excitement and were proud of what they would share on
their missions.

On their daily mountaintop lesson, the King announced,
"Today you will learn about sharing what you know with
others." With another wave of his hands, the Royal Family
found themselves in the smaller kingdom.

This time, they were in a building of some sort, differ-
ent from the buildings in their kingdom. The buildings in
the smaller kingdom seemed to have a covering, just like the
beings that live there.

The buildings in the Kingdom of Light are surrounded
by a glow of clear light. There are no walls; you can see

the outside through the clear light. The outside seems to be inside the building and the inside seems to be the outside too. Here, in this smaller kingdom, you can only see what's outside through the openings called windows.

"They are called 'walls,'" the Queen answered their unspoken question and then she continued, "There are no walls in our Kingdom, because there is no separation of the outside from the inside. All is Light and all is one."

The children then turned their attention to what was happening within the walls of this building. They were in a music room. They also saw the Angees. There were several musical instruments and some people were playing and some were being taught how to play.

Gi immediately went to a piano as he watched a young girl playing the musical notes. She was playing a musical piece and seemed to be having trouble with it as her teacher was saying, "Keep practicing." The young girl kept hitting the wrong keys and each time she missed the keys, the Shadow seem to get larger around her and she looked like she wanted to run away.

Her Guardian Angee was standing next to her and seemed to be sending Light into her. Then the girl stopped and looked up and said something so softly as if she was whispering. Gi was standing next to her and he heard her whisper as if she was talking to someone, "Why can't I get this right? Please help me."

Immediately a Messenger Angee appeared and whispered something in the young girl's ear.

PK, who was standing next to the Queen and King couldn't hear what Gi could hear and the Queen gently explained to the Princess, "She just asked for help and the Music Experts from our kingdom heard her and the Messenger Angee was sent to give her what she is asking for. Help is always given. It is up to the being to be open and receive it."

The young girl heard the guidance from the Messenger Angee and she sat up straight and played the music beautifully.

The teacher heard it and walked back to her and said, "Now you've got it!"

Many Angees suddenly appeared and they were applauding and the young girl kept on smiling as she completed her piece. When she was playing she was glowing and the Shadow disappeared. "She is feeling joy!" exclaimed PK and the King nodded.

When Gi joined his family, PK asked, "What was the Messenger Angee whispering?"

Gi said, "The Angee was telling her which keys to hit and was saying, 'feel the music from within.'"

Pleased with what the children had learned, the King said proudly, "That is sharing. When you lovingly and willingly share your gifts and talents, you are teaching others to also share their own special gifts and talents bringing forth the joy that is within. When joy is present the Shadow departs." The Angees waved goodbye to the Royal Family as the King waved his hands and they left the music school.

With another wave of his hands, the Royal Family found themselves in another building called a hospital. Here the children saw something that they had never seen before. "This is called pain and suffering," the Queen explained to the children. "The beings come here for help from the doctors to take away their pain and their suffering."

The King and the Queen explained that the covering, called the body, is necessary for a Light Being in order for them to live in this kingdom. The body is exposed to so much Shadow that it experiences the feeling of pain, the opposite of joy. The King explained that "The doctors in this hospital are given the talents to help remove the pain and heal the suffering so these beings can again remember to feel joy."

The children saw what pain and suffering looks like. They also saw lights coming from the doctors and others that were there to help. They saw many Angees in this building standing beside those who were in pain.

The children also saw that some beings were happy and leaving the hospital and some were sleeping peacefully. They saw many who were surrounded by brilliant violet lights that they hadn't seen before and the Angees were smiling at them.

"What are they doing?" asked Gi. "They are praying," answered the Queen. "This is a way to connect with the Light within that reaches into our kingdom at the same time. Those lights of prayer are connected directly to our Light and we hear and know what their needs are. Right now they are connecting to our light and our light gives them the healing they need. Remember always that no being here is ever alone. They each have their own Guardian Angee, they constantly have access to the Talent Experts from the Kingdom of Light for inspiration and sharing with others, but more importantly, each being here knows that we are here to help them on the journey and all they need to do is connect to their Light, which is also my Light, within them. We know what their needs are and we are always ready to guide them and show them the truth of who they are. It is only when they acknowledge the presence of the Light within and go there that all good things, things of Light, show up and the Shadow disappears."

The children watched as the King and Queen moved to stand next to those who were surrounded by the brilliant violet light and they placed their hands on their heads. The Angees sang and applauded and the lights got brighter and brighter all around. They knew that the pain and suffering had disappeared. The shadows were gone.

The Royal Family left and returned to their mountaintop having learned more about sharing their gifts and talents.

PK had been quiet during their visit to the hospital and she announced, "I want to be just like those doctors and help take away the pain and suffering. How can I do that?" she asked the King and Queen.

The King and Queen both laughed. The King said "Little One, you are already doing that. Your interest is in learning about the plants, flowers, and trees that contain the medicines needed to repair and restore the body, and these medicines take away much of the pain and suffering that you just saw today. That is what you will be sharing with the smaller kingdom."

The Princess was deep in thought. She then looked at her brother, who was smiling at her, as if he could hear her thoughts, and then she looked at the King and Queen and solemnly announced, "I want to go to the smaller kingdom and bring my talents to help remove all their pain and suffering. That is how I want to share what I already know and what I am still learning. That place really needs joy and I know I can do it."

The King and Queen smiled at PK and they both nodded in agreement to her decision. The Princess hugged them all. She had decided to make the journey too.

The King then addressed both his children and said, "Learn all you can from the Talent Experts and the Learning Masters here and that is what you will share with others in the smaller kingdom."

The children understood their lesson in sharing and once again the King placed his hands on top of their heads so they would always remember their lesson on sharing.

Brian stopped speaking and Karen looked at him and they both nodded. It was now time for the group to get ready for bed. Brian told the group waiting to hear more, "That's it for tonight, kids."

"No! We want to hear more!" they all protested.

"We will continue the story tomorrow. Now that you know that both of the Royal children have decided to make the journey, tomorrow we'll tell you how they are prepared for this courageous journey and how they get to choose the lives they want to live," Karen assured them.

Kay asked, "They get to choose any life they want?"

"Yes. The choice that they make will be the perfect choice for them to use their talents and fulfill their mission." Brian responded.

"Does she take the horse with her?" asked Jo. Lee immediately jumped and asked, "And the dolphin, too?" The two girls giggled.

The grandparents laughed along with them and got the group to get ready for bed and move to their assigned sleeping quarters.

The Secret Exposed

WHEN THE GRANDCHILDREN WERE safely in their different rooms, Karen and Brian cleaned up and enjoyed a cup of tea while they discussed the success of the birthday plans. Karen was happy that her one birthday wish—to share their knowledge with their grandchildren—was coming true. She was indeed happy and content. *It has been the best birthday ever*, she thought.

Little did they know that Corina was making her way to the kitchen to get a drink of water and managed to overhear the last part of their conversation.

"Did you notice the glimpses of light that appeared on and off while we were telling them about the Kingdom?" Karen asked Brian.

Brian nodded, "Yes, I did. I think the Angees were applauding our storytelling talent."

"Hey, is that one of our talents, you think?" Karen laughed and she stood up and hugged her cousin, her best friend, her prince brother, "Goodnight, Prince Branigi."

"Good night, PK," Brian answered as he kissed his cousin, his best friend, and his princess sister, on her cheek.

"Oh!" Corina gasped, and she quickly put her hand over her mouth and ran back to her room before she was discovered. Corina climbed into her bed quietly so she wouldn't disturb her sleeping cousins and little sister. She lay on her bed trying to fathom what she had just heard. Her grandfather was the Prince and her Aunt Karen was the Princess! She then smiled to herself and snuggled deeper into the covers and happily went to sleep.

The next morning, the group got up and prepared for another day of fun in the sun. The plans were breakfast, playing on the beach, and then walking into town where they kids could decide which junk food they wanted to eat and do some last minute shopping before the birthday cake celebration scheduled for the evening. Corina was especially quiet that morning and stayed very close to her grandfather.

Corina finally found the perfect time to talk to her grandfather and her Aunt Karen. Brian and Karen were sitting alone while the group scattered throughout the little shops in town. Corina joined them and before either one could ask why she wasn't looking in the shops with the others, she blurted out her question, "Are you Prince Gi and PK? I heard you talking last night. I didn't mean to eavesdrop, I just wanted to get a drink and I heard you talking." She then stopped to catch her breath, she had been holding this in all morning and she thought she would burst if she didn't say anything.

Brian lovingly put his arms around his granddaughter and with a quick glance at Karen's look of approval, he said, "Yes, we are."

Corina hugged her grandfather and her aunt and said "What about the others, shall we tell them?"

"I don't think we need to do that, dear. I have a feeling that they will all figure it by themselves," Karen assured her.

Brian explained as tenderly as he could to his young granddaughter, "You see, Corina, the story is not only about the Prince and the Princess, it's about how everyone who is here is here for a purpose, for a mission. We wanted to spend this time with all of you because Aunt Karen and I realize how important it is that we impart this to our grandchildren."

"But why didn't you tell us about all this sooner? All this time I never knew that my grandfather and my favorite aunt are royalty," Corina asked, truly wanting to understand.

Karen lovingly smiled at her niece and said, "Corina, we are all royalty. We all come from the same place. Like your grandfather said earlier, us telling you this is not to draw attention to the Prince and Princess but to draw attention to what it is you want to do, share, and teach to others to bring out their Light and to be in touch with your own Light. When you hear the rest of the story tonight, you will see how we, the Royal children, were prepared just like all the others to decide how to accomplish our mission. Then you might understand that all of us are on a mission, including the King and Queen."

Corina nodded. Brian then addressed her question as to why they were just being told this.

"Your Aunt Karen and I have always had a 'feeling' that we were here for a purpose, but we were not given the glimpse of our beginnings until just recently. We certainly didn't know that we were Gi and PK. We don't understand why this happened, but we both feel that we need to share what we have been shown about this place called the Kingdom of Light with our grandchildren. This is our gift to you so you may know at an earlier age."

"Thank you Grandfather, thank you, Aunt Karen, for sharing all this," Corina solemnly said and with one more hug, she went off to find the others, pleased with herself that she had a private audience.

Brian called after her, "Corina, round everybody up, it's time to go back."

⌒ The Masters ⌒

THE GROUP RETURNED TO the beach house after a fun-filled afternoon of playing, eating, and shopping. There was a surprise waiting for Karen. She knew who was responsible when she saw the delectable platters of food that Lola had prepared, including a beautifully decorated birthday cake. Brian had Trevor smuggle all the goods into the house while they were in town. Everything looked so delicious and festive. Karen took the time to call her dear friend and tearfully thanked her.

After the eating and sharing of their afternoon, the group sang "Happy Birthday" to Karen and took dozens of pictures to share with their parents. Gifts were opened and Karen loved everything she was given. Everyone was enjoying themselves, and since it was their last night of reunion, they talked about doing it again.

Then the evening turned to storytelling time. The group could hardly wait to see how the story ended.

So, once again, they took their respective places and settled in.

Brian began.

Prince Branigi was now ready to attend the School of Learning to be prepared for his journey into the smaller kingdom. PK would continue to learn from the Art and Medicine Experts until it was her time.

The Masters in the School of Learning prepared the Light Beings for the life in the smaller kingdom. Gi's friends, Trevori and Joni, were also in the School of Learning, and together they got prepared for their mission.

Gi had been studying marine life with the Marine Experts and learning from the Music Experts. Joni had been studying with the Art Experts; he wanted to share the beauty of lights and colors. He also had been studying with the Law Experts. He had been taught the different laws that govern the smaller kingdom and felt very strongly that he could help change some of those laws to make life easier.

Trevori wanted to make people laugh and was always creating gadgets as fun toys. When the boys were younger, Trevori would create gadgets as fun toys and the three of them would rush off to show them to Hecri of the Toy and Gadget Shoppe. Some of his ideas were sent to the smaller kingdom and hundreds of children there enjoyed his fun toys. He, also, had been sharing his talent with those in the smaller kingdoms. Eager for their journey, the three friends agreed that they would leave for their mission at the same time.

On their first day at the School of Learning, the Learning Masters, surrounded by brilliant red and gold lights, explained to the class, "In this School of Learning, you will be shown how the beings in the smaller kingdom live. How they begin their journey as small babies learning to walk and talk and become like the beings there. It is not at all like living here. Over there, you will have to live with both the Light and the Shadow. Here we will show you how the beings live when they are connected to their Light and how beings live who have lost their connection to the Light and are surrounded by the Shadow.

"You will also be shown how the Light Beings from here are constantly sending help and reminders of who you are and your mission."

The Masters continued, "The smaller kingdom is like a classroom. There you will become a student and a teacher. As a student, you will learn how to live with others, you will learn what opposites feel like. You will make choices on your journey. Some of those choices will bring more Shadow or more Light.

"You will also be teachers on your journey. You will teach others how to find their own Light. You will do this by using your talents, the gifts that the King and Queen have lovingly given you. Each talent is unique and no two talents are alike because each being shares that talent in a different way. It is very important that these talents are shared. Doing so brings more Light into that kingdom. Each being whom you will meet is also a student and a teacher. You will always be learning and always be teaching.

"Everything that you see there will teach you something about who you are. You will see this in a flower, a tree, the animals, the oceans, the sun, the rain, the sky, the moon, and the stars. Even those things that may not seem to be a beautiful and joyful creation will also teach you about the existence of the Shadow. The Light within will gently remind you that you choose what you wish to learn while you are there. As you grow you will be guided by your Guardian Angee to meet others who will lead you to express and expand your chosen talents and chosen role to fulfill your mission."

⮑ Life in the Smaller Kingdom ⮐

BRIAN PAUSED AT THIS point of the story and allowed Karen to continue.

The Masters then asked the class to turn their attention to the big screen. The class watched as a Light Being walked through a thin veil and came out the other side as a newborn baby with a body.

The class saw the newborn let out a loud cry and the inner light from the baby was bursting out in all different directions. The Masters explained that it is initially a shock to the Light Being to find itself in a strange body and in a strange environment, but the initial shock passes. It is crying because it is trying to express itself but is unable to because it does not yet know how to communicate.

They continued to explain that in order to live in the smaller kingdom, each being who entered must take upon itself a body made of flesh and bones. Each being chose the body and the life they would live in that body. They must take care of the body they selected. Their body was what would take them to where they needed to be to continue to live there to share their talents and gifts. Once the journey was complete, they would leave the body behind and the Light Being would return here.

The students continued to watch and laugh as they saw how the Light within a small baby reached out and touched all those around it, making them laugh and act playful.

The Masters explained, "From this big screen, you will be allowed to see through the body so you may see and understand how the inner Light of the being responds to its new environment and to the others."

The class then saw the lights come from the parents of the baby and go directly into the baby. The class then saw how the light from the baby seemed to reach out to the lights coming from the parents and soon it looked like the lights were dancing with each other.

The baby stopped crying and the parents smiled and their lights became brighter and brighter, filling up the whole room. "That is the beginning of those three beings bonding with each. There is joy and trust being exchanged," the Masters explained.

The Masters then explained that the moment that baby came into that kingdom, the mission began. Because the Light Being was still connected to this place, it was still filled with joy and that joy was the light that came from the baby and instantly touched the Light of joy that was in everyone there. Whenever that Light of joy was touched, a smile formed. That is why everyone smiled at a newborn baby.

In the next scene, the class witnessed how the baby grew and how its lights were affected. They saw how the light expanded and danced with the lights of family members and that more bonds with those beings were being formed.

They also saw the baby cry when it was hungry and how its Guardian Angee would sing a soft song making the baby smile.

The Masters further explained, "Just as everything here has its own music, each being has its own music coming from its inner Light. Just as you are seeing through the body to see the Light, you will also hear the music. This music vibrates at a certain frequency that responds to another's frequency and their lights dance together. This is how Light Beings attract each other. The beings who continue to connect to their inner Light vibrate similar frequencies and they instantly reach out to each other.

"The beings who choose to surround themselves with the Shadow vibrate a different frequency and they also attract the beings surrounded by the Shadow, but a being connected to the Light and a being surrounded by Shadow vibrate at different frequencies, their music does not match, and their lights do not dance together, therefore, they repel each other."

The students turned their attention once again to the screen and watched as the baby continued to expand its light and its music as it learned new and fun things in its environment. However, when the baby experienced pain, the brilliance of the light became dull and the happy uplifting vibration of its music changed to a different tempo.

As the students watched this happen, the Masters explained, "That is the Shadow making its appearance. The being is now experiencing something that is not of the Light."

The baby's mother appeared and put a drop of liquid into the baby's ears. After a few minutes, the crying stopped and the baby's light burst through and the dullness became bright again and the music changed to its happy uplifting vibration.

The Masters explained, "There, the pain in the ears has stopped, the baby returns to its joy, and the Shadow and its vibration disappears."

"Wow!" the students exclaimed, and the room was filled with applause, including the applause of the Angees who seemed to appear out of nowhere, and now surrounded the baby and filled the room with more light.

The students watched the various stages of growth and saw how the Shadow surrounded the being in moments of pain, anger, resentment, and sadness and the Shadow remained until the being experienced joy, laughter, sharing, and love. In these moments, the inner Light burst through the Shadow, and like magic, the Shadow retreated.

The Masters explained, "You see that it is only when the being chooses to stay in the pain, anger, resentment, or sadness that the Shadow remains and the being attracts more of the same. This is how so many beings who leave here forget that they are Light Beings because all that seems to show up on their journeys are more shadows, but this is because they themselves are attracting more shadows."

They watched another scene of a young boy and a young girl playing and a Guardian Angee always there protecting them from harm. They were also shown scenes where the younger beings could hear the music from the trees and the mountains while the older ones could no longer hear them.

They were also shown scenes where one being helped another, just as the Prince witnessed on one of their trips to the smaller kingdom with his family. The class applauded as they saw how the light got brighter and brighter. Those beings had not forgotten their Light within.

At the end of that first day, Gi and his friends and several other students talked excitedly about how they were going to help those who had forgotten who they were. That day, Gi shared with PK what he learned and what he saw. The King and Queen stood and watched and listened as both their children shared what they would do on their mission.

Karen stopped speaking to allow this part of the story to sink in. The grandchildren were quiet for a few seconds, and then they started talking all at once.

"So, this is the smaller kingdom, isn't it?" Nigel asked.

"Didn't you figure that out already?" Shane responded smiling at his young cousin.

"Well, I guess I did, but now I'm sure," replied Nigel.

"Me, too," answered both Lee and Jo.

Kay asked very quietly as if in a whisper, "Is that right, G-ma? We all come from the Kingdom of Light?"

Karen looked at her oldest grandchild, knowing that she already knew the answer to that question and replied, "What do you think?"

Kay looked at her grandmother and smiled and said, "It does sound and feel familiar to me. Every time you and Uncle Brian describe the place, it's like I've been there; I could see the lights you talk about and how happy everyone is in that place. It just feels so natural, so organic, somehow. At first, it didn't make sense to me, but now it does make a lot of sense. So, does that mean that I've been getting glimpses of that kingdom? In some parts of the story, I get goose bumps all over."

Everyone began talking all at once again and they were saying, "Me, too, I get the goose bumps!" and "I get goose bumps, too!" Then they started talking about and sharing which part of the story gave them more goose bumps.

Brian quieted down the group so they could hear more of what the Masters of the School of Learning shared with the group before they were prepared to leave.

Every Being Has a Purpose

B RIAN THEN CONTINUED WITH the story.
The Masters explained to the students how each being
had a purpose in the smaller kingdom and instructed the students to turn their attention to the big screen so they could
witness what was happening right at that moment in the
other place.

The class saw workers building what was explained as
houses for the beings to live in and roads for the beings to
travel on. "While you are there in your new bodies, you
will need vehicles called automobiles, trains, boats, ships,
and airplanes to get to other places. Unlike this place where
you get to one place or another by simply thinking yourself
there, in the smaller kingdom you will need these things," the
Masters explained.

They saw doctors and nurses in a hospital scene. They
saw scenes of other doctors and nurses with animals. They
saw speakers speaking to great numbers of beings in different buildings, some in classrooms, some in churches, some in
large buildings. Some speakers were speaking into what was

explained as a camera. The students saw that thousands of beings were watching and listening from a screen in their homes. Whatever message they were saying on the screen, many were listening to them. They saw groups of beings in a building working with different equipment. They saw beings preparing meals for other beings. They saw beings stocking items in shops and stores and other beings coming in to purchase them. They saw beings making clothes and shoes. They saw beings building furniture. They saw beings playing musical instruments and singing. They saw beings painting beautiful artwork.

In each scene, they saw the presence of the Guardian Angees. Some scenes showed Messenger Angees delivering messages from this side, and they saw Angees applauding and filling the space with more light when the beings were expressing their talents for others to enjoy.

The Masters showed the students how important joy, laughter, and love was, living in the smaller kingdom. They were shown scenes of parents and their children laughing, talking, playing, and eating with each together. Parents were teaching their children how to walk and talk, how to eat, how to read, how to dress, and how to play. They saw their lights expanding and their inner music playing together. These scenes were filled with lights and the Angees applauding.

The Masters explained, "All of you will choose who your parents will be before you enter that kingdom, and you will also be taught by the parents you have chosen. The first lessons you will learn are about love and laughter, and from these two things, you will feel the joy that is the magic within you. Some of you will grow and become parents, too, and you will teach those beings who show up as your children. Those who are to become your children have also chosen you."

More scenes were shown of beings laughing and playing together. There were families and friends having fun on the beach, surfing, swimming, or throwing a ball around.

Gi could see the dolphins playing in the water. The beings didn't seem to see them. The dolphins were too far out. Gi pointed to the dolphins and his friends could see them too.

There were scenes of a being on a stage making the audience laugh. Trevori especially loved these scenes. "That is what I'm going to do," he whispered to Gi and Joni, and his friends both nodded knowing that he would be good at his talent of making others laugh.

Then there were scenes of competition in sports. The students cheered and applauded as they watched beings racing in their cars and scenes of beings playing other sports. The three friends especially loved the football and the basketball scenes as they cheered the players on.

Excited about what they learned that day in school, the students sought the Talent Experts to learn about the talents they would bring on their mission. Gi, Joni, and Trevori headed for the beach. They called their dolphins and obediently the dolphins swam to them and off they went riding and playing in the water and throwing the ball to each other. After they were done playing with their friends from the deep, the boys lay on the beach and Gi said, "I'm going to teach the beings in the smaller kingdom how to talk to the dolphins and play with them."

Trevori said, "I'm going to make them laugh. I'm going to make fun things and games that will make them laugh."

Joni said, "I'm going to learn the laws of the land, change them, and play sports." The boys also talked about being the best fathers for their children.

The boys were not aware that the King and Queen were watching and listening. The King and Queen smiled at each other knowing that these three friends would indeed bring more Light into the smaller kingdom.

PK Goes to the
⌒ School of Learning ⌒

B RIAN STOPPED SPEAKING AND Karen stood up
and announced, "Before I continue with the story
about the Princess and her friends going to the School
of Learning, do you kids want to take a short break?"

Karen and Brian were both startled at the unani-
mous and definite "No!" that came from all the kids.
So, Karen sat back down again and continued.

*Now it was time for PK and her friends to attend the
School of Learning. The girls had talked about what talents
they would share with others and had been learning from the
Talent Experts in the kingdom. Now they were ready to be
taught by the Learning Masters about what to expect once
they enter the smaller kingdom.*

*PK and her friends listened to the Masters explain their
mission and watched the big screen, just as Gi and his friends
had done and they showed the same scenes. As PK watched
the hospital scenes, she knew that this was her mission, to
help the bodies get stronger and to help others vanquish their
shadows by relieving their pain and their suffering.*

Shajula was especially interested in the clothes that the beings were wearing. She wanted to help design the clothes and help create fun things to wear on their heads and their feet.

Brilola especially enjoyed watching the scenes of the artists. She wanted to help bring more beauty and light into that kingdom through painting and all kinds of artwork. All the girls enjoyed watching the scenes of parents and teachers helping the young children.

After each day at the School of Learning, PK and her friends met with their Talent Experts. All three friends met with the Experts in charge of bringing beauty into the smaller kingdom. They learned about gardening and the different types of flowers and plants that grew there. They learned which flowers and plants brought beauty and which ones were used to help heal the bodies of the beings there. They learned how a painting could bring joy to those who saw it.

Since all three friends loved animals, they also learned about the lives of the horses, cats, and dogs in the smaller kingdom and how to care for, play, and listen to them. PK said, "I'm going to have a horse and a dog when I get there."

Shajula and Brilola both wanted to have a horse, too, but each preferred the idea of a cat as their pet. The girls went to their favorite place, the field of flowers, and as they were making crowns of flowers to wear on their heads, they talked and talked about what they learned and saw that day. They agreed that they would meet each other and remind each other of their mission in the smaller kingdom.

Then PK summoned Wings and the three girls mounted the beautiful white horse and off they went up into the sky, flying, laughing with their hair flying in the wind and their crowns of flowers with twinkling lights. The townspeople could hear their laughter and waved as the horse flew up. The King and Queen watched their daughter and her friends having fun and laughing. The King and Queen smiled knowing that these three friends would indeed bring the magic of joy, love, and laughter into the Kingdom of Opposites.

Save the Kingdom of Opposites

BRIAN CONTINUED THE STORY.
On the last day of school, all students of the School of Learning were gathered into one big class as the Masters explained an important mission that they would do together as a group. Gi and PK and their friends sat together to listen to this important mission.

As they watched the scene before them of what was happening right at the moment in the smaller kingdom, the class saw how parts of that kingdom were being destroyed. They watched as lighted parts of a forest were being destroyed by equipment that was cutting down the trees. They watched beings setting fire to the beautiful forest, killing the trees, flowers, and birds in the area.

They were shown how the Shadow surrounding these beings was like a dark murky gray color and they could hear the harsh tempo of their music. They watched as the air filled with smoke from the fires that were killing the birds and making so many beings sick from breathing the air. They watched as the Shadow covered so many of these once lighted places. The class could hear the trees, the flowers, and the birds crying.

They also watched as beings dumped things into the oceans, killing the fish and plant life that lived in the water.

"The Kingdom of Opposites is being slowly destroyed by those beings who have forgotten their mission to save it. When the shadows surround these once lighted and magical places, only more Shadow will come for greater destruction," one Learning Master explained.

Then the class was shown what the Learning Master meant by greater destruction. They saw huge waves come up from the oceans and wash away everything in their path. They saw houses being swept away and beings trying to run from the huge waves, but the waves overtook them. They were shown the ground moving and shaking as homes, roads, cars, animals, and beings fell and died.

They were shown the destruction of powerful winds that blew away homes, trees, and everything in their path. They saw how fast and destructive a fire could be, killing everything in its path, they saw how so much rain could flood an area, drowning all who live there, and they also saw how a place could dry up and die without any rain.

The Masters continued, "Everything in the Kingdom of Opposites is created to be in balance and in harmony. The sun, the wind, and the rain each have a part in the balance and harmony; too much of one thing will destroy the balance.

"The fires are meant to cook the food or to keep you warm; too much fire will destroy the balance. The air surrounding that kingdom is meant to be clean so the bodies can breathe it in and continue on their journey; too much of what is not clean will pollute the air and the bodies cannot breathe and the bodies will die.

"The living things in the oceans, lakes, and rivers and the living things in the forest have enough food and air to live and breathe until the beings fill their place with unclean air, which takes away their foods and means that they will also die. All this destruction creates only more shadows and the balance and harmony is broken and more shadows take over creating more destruction to the Kingdom of Opposites."

The class was then shown scenes of beings destroying each other. They saw scenes of war where the beings used weapons to destroy each other.

The Masters explained, "Here you see that again the balance and harmony to exist with each other is destroyed. These beings have forgotten that they are brothers and sisters with a mission to help, share, and live with each other, so they end up destroying each other because they want what the other one has."

In all the scenes from the destruction of the parts of the kingdom and the destruction of each other, there were hundreds of Angees all around whispering to those doing the destruction and comforting those in pain. "What are they whispering?" one of the students asked and the Master answered, "They are saying, 'Be the Light.'"

The Masters continued, "Just as the Shadow comes, the Light also will come. The beings who remember their mission show up as the Light to help those living things and beings in trouble."

In the forest burning in the fire, they saw beings surrounded by lights putting out the fire with large hoses of water and they saw these beings surrounded by their Guardian Angees who were protecting and guiding them. Some of the students in the class who were seeing this scene silently declared that they would help save the forests as part of their mission.

In the scene that showed beings tumbling and falling as the ground was moving and shaking, other beings were shown helping them get to shelter and caring for their pain. In the scene of the forest being cut and the waters and air being filled with pollution, there were many scenes of beings talking to the leaders of the place to stop filling the waters and air with the pollution that was killing the kingdom.

In each of these scenes the Guardian Angees and the Messenger Angees were whispering "Be the Light." Some listened and some could not hear the words being whispered. The class saw that those who listened were surrounded by the Light that came from within and it grew brighter and brighter and the Angees applauded. Those who did not hear were attracting more Shadow.

Some in the class vowed silently that they would become a leader who would stop the destruction, and some vowed that they would be the one to speak to the leaders of the smaller kingdom to stop the destruction.

In the scenes of war, the class was shown how the leaders of the different parts of that kingdom decided to declare war or decided to declare peace with their neighbors. Again, as in each scene the Angees surrounded the leaders whispering, "Be the Light," and again some listened and some did not hear, for they had forgotten their mission to stop the fighting.

Every single one of the Light Beings in the class silently vowed, "I will be the Light when I get there."

In all these scenes the class also saw how the power of the Light is spread to stop the destruction. They saw scenes of beings surrounded by violet lights gathering together in small groups and in large groups palms put together or just bowing connecting to their Light from within and sending their Light to the places around the kingdom that were in need. The class saw how the Light spread far and wide and saw that as the Light touched another being, their own Light within seemed to light up and spread wider.

The Masters explained, "Those beings are connecting to the Light within and are asking for our help. When our help is needed, we show up to help." The class saw thousands of Angees clearing the way for the Light to reach millions of others.

"That is the magic and the power of the Light that each one of you always carries within you. When your Light clears away the Shadow, you will also send your Light to clear another's Shadow, and then they will hear the whisper, 'Be the Light,' and the Light shall win the battle with the Shadow."

In the other scenes they were shown how the shadow of destruction began. They had previously seen the scenes of parents teaching, laughing, and playing with children, and now they were shown parents and children fighting with each other, attracting the Shadow around them and vibrating harsh tempos.

These children grew up living in this shadow of fear and continued to surround their lives with more fear and more shadow. They attracted other beings who were also living in fear.

They had forgotten that there was a magical Light within and they had forgotten their mission. They did not hear the whispers of their Guardian Angee. The students saw how many others showed up on their journey as teachers to teach the beings to be the Light and again these beings living in shadow did not hear. They ended up becoming those beings who brought destruction to the place and to themselves.

They also saw how some of the beings changed when they remembered who they were or when another's light touched their Light within and they could finally hear the whispers of their Guardian Angees to use their talents and gifts to bring more light to the place. They saw how the Shadow disappeared instantly and their way of life changed from Shadow to Light. Everyone in the class applauded at this scene.

The Masters explained, "All beings in the smaller kingdom are just like each one of you here. They all came from here and they all saw the scenes of the destruction of the Shadow and the peace and joy from the Light. Each being also said that they would never forget their mission but sadly, many do."

Brian paused in this part of the story and waited for the kids to say something. For the second time, since they began telling the story of the Kingdom of Light, the children were quiet. They did not talk all at once or clown around as they had before.

Karen and Brian waited knowing that the seeds were now truly planted in their minds and hearts. They all had a mission during their time here.

Nigel was the first one to speak up, "I think I now understand why I'm interested in studying political science when I go to college. I am going to be a leader of the Light and help save this place."

"I am going into journalism," Corina announced, "and I'm going to write or broadcast to everyone that we need to save this place and ourselves."

Kay said, "I'm going to use my law degree to help those who need my help and to punish those who break the law."

Shane, who was usually the one who spoke up first, was quiet. He was deep in thought. He was thinking of ways to help stop the destruction. He finally said, "I think I'm going to design buildings that are safe for people."

Lee looked at everyone and said, "I'm going to help too." Jo said, "I don't like to hear that they made the birds, trees, and fishes cry. I don't like that!" Jo's statement made everyone laugh and soon the somber atmosphere became one of determination to be a part of the mission. Once again, everyone started talking at the same time.

The Gifts

KAREN QUIETED THE GROUP once more and continued with the story.

The class had a lot to think about after seeing the destruction of the smaller kingdom, and after the Masters finished speaking, the King and Queen made their appearance to the class.

Everyone knew that something very important was about to happen.

The King spoke, "You have now been taught by the Masters here and you have all been shown what life will be like in the smaller kingdom and now you must make a choice. No one here can make you leave and go to the smaller kingdom. You can choose to remain here and help that kingdom from here or you can journey into the Kingdom of Opposites to live among the shadows and bring into that place more of your Light. If you choose to make your journey there, you will choose how you will complete your mission of bringing Light into that place and once your mission is completed you will return home."

Everyone in the class said they would continue on into the smaller kingdom. This pleased the King and Queen.

The Queen then spoke, "You will take with you your own lights of love, joy, laughter, and beauty, but before you leave this place, we will bestow upon each of you additional special lights of power. These lights are that of courage, strength, wisdom, gentleness, and creation. These new lights have power over the Shadow because these are our lights. You will always take a part of us with you on your journey. The King and I will always be with you and you will know us and feel our presence whenever you access those special gifts and you will come to know the full power of their magic."

The Royal Rulers spread their arms and their lights filled the room and surrounded each student. Soon each student was immersed in millions of twinkling lights and they all clapped and laughed. They had just been given some of the King and Queen's lights.

The Queen continued, "The more you use these new power lights, the more you will come to know compassion, understanding, gratitude, appreciation, forgiveness, and peace. These new gifts will bring more joy and more laughter and love on your journey.

You will need these gifts because when you begin your journey in the smaller kingdom, you will begin to forget this place and learn to live as beings of that kingdom.

When you sometimes feel like you are all alone and feel lost on the journey, you will be given glimpses of our kingdom and it will feel familiar to you. In these moments you connect to us and to all the Light Beings in this kingdom."

The King then explained, "The opposite of these lights is the shadow called fear. Fear brings the shadows of anger, greed, blame, disappointment, grief, resentment, jealousy, guilt, and sadness. When you choose fear, you will feel disconnected from us and disconnected from your lights. The longer you stay with these feelings the more you disconnect from the source of your magical power. We cannot force you to use the power of your lights even though it is always there. You are free to choose. That is our greatest gift of all, the gift of free will."

Then it was time for each one to tell the King and Queen how they would accomplish their mission. As each student solemnly declared their intention, the King and Queen lovingly placed their hands on them and their talents were given. Many different talents were given that day. The talents to lead, to speak, to build, to teach, to write, to paint, to sing, to dance, to play music, to heal, to nurse, to feed, to shelter, to bring laughter, to entertain, to nurture, to protect, and so much more.

Everyone chose to help stop the destruction of that kingdom through their chosen mission. Each one declared that through their chosen role they would "Be the Light."

The Royal Rulers left the class with these parting words, "Some of your chosen roles will seem difficult and hard on your journey because you will have forgotten where you came from. Remember to go within during those difficult times and there we will be for you and you will know that you have nothing to fear, you are all children of Light."

The final class was over and everyone had so much to think about and everyone was so excited about their own mission. They shared amongst themselves what part they should play to accomplish their mission. They also made agreements to meet each other on their journey and remind each other of why they were there.

ᕫ The Journey Begins ᕭ

KAREN CONTINUED WITH THE STORY.
After they completed the School of Learning, each student continued their learning with the Talent Experts until it was time for them to make their entrance into the smaller kingdom.

The Prince chose to be a scientist in the smaller kingdom to learn and protect the oceans and the forests. He also chose to bring the music of this kingdom into the smaller kingdom. He would learn music and then help teach others to bring it into their lives.

PK chose to help heal those in need of healing. She chose to learn medicine and the use of plants to help those bodies who were suffering. She also chose to use her talents in art to bring light and beauty through her painting.

Gi and PK's friends chose how they would use their talents to complete their mission and all made a pact to meet each other and remind each other of the mission.

At their daily mountaintop lesson, the Royal Family talked about the journey they would soon begin. The King and Queen were very pleased with their children's choices of their roles. That day they traveled to many places in the smaller kingdom and were asked to choose where they would like to live when they began their journey.

Gi said that he wanted to live near water so he could learn about the oceans and how to protect those who live there. PK said that she wanted to live where there were horses and fields of flowers.

The Prince talked about teaching the beings to hear the music of the whales and to hear the sounds of the dolphins. "If the beings could hear what I could hear, they would never again put anything in the oceans to destroy those beautiful animals and I'm going to make sure of that! If they could only hear the beautiful music from the trees in the forest, they would never again destroy them, and I'm going to make sure of that, too!" Everyone laughed because they know that if anyone could accomplish this mission, Prince Gi could.

PK talked about what she had been learning from the Medical Experts in the kingdom. "I'm going to share and teach all that I've learned about the use of plants as medicine and I'm going to heal those who are sick and teach them the power of their Light within and I'm going to be an artist and paint beautiful pictures of flowers and sunsets and I'm going to plant sunflowers!!"

The brother and sister also talked about their role as parents and they agreed that they would pass the knowledge of the magical Light to the beings who would choose them as their mother and their father. The King and Queen listened quietly knowing that there would be times when the Royal children would have to battle many shadows before their missions were complete.

The time has come for the Prince to choose his parents and begin the journey that awaited him. He wanted to become a scientist. He also wanted to bring the gift of joy in music. And he chose to begin his journey near the ocean. The parents he chose to learn from were both teachers. The father taught science at a local college and the mother was a music teacher for younger children. He would be their first and only child. The Prince made several visits to his chosen parents as they awaited his arrival.

His chosen mother could sense him when he visited and she would smile lovingly at her husband and say, "It's going to be a boy and he is going to be very smart."

"How would you know that he's going to be smart?" the husband teased her, and his wife just smiled and said, "I just know."

Gi spent his last few days with his two closest friends. They played with their dolphins and Gi told Sergie that he'd be back soon and he would never forget him. The three friends also played a lot of basketball and football and made plans as to how they would recognize each other when they met on the journey. They agreed that when they went to the beach, they would remember each other, especially if they saw a dolphin. Gi would leave first and Trevori and Joni would follow soon after.

Trevori had chosen a family that needed joy and laughter. The mother was very pretty and stayed home to care for two daughters. She seemed to be tired all the time. The father was a mechanic, always working under the hood of a car or fixing things around the small farmhouse. The family was poor and there was no laughter in that home. Trevori said, "I shall bring laughter and joy into that home!"

Gi said, "It's not going to be an easy life; are you sure that's where you want to be?"

Trevori said, "Yes. I will make my new mother laugh and I could learn a lot from my new father about cars, and I may teach him about making new gadgets for the car."

Joni and Gi both laughed knowing that he would definitely bring more joy and laughter into that family.

Joni had chosen a family that lived not too far from the family that Trevori had chosen. The father was a teacher at the local high school and the mother worked as a nurse at the hospital. Joni knew that he could learn a lot from both parents. Joni and Trevori would make their journey only a few days apart. They would both meet in high school and become best friends. It would be much later that they would meet with the Prince at the beach as they had agreed.

Then it was time for Prince Gi to meet his Guardian Angee. As the final moments came before Gi was to make his entrance into the smaller kingdom, the King and Queen reminded him once again that they would always be there with him. He did not feel sad that he was leaving the Kingdom of Light because he knew that once his mission was complete he would return.

PK was happy for her brother and she said to him, "You won't forget me because I'll be there visiting you every day and playing with you until it's my time to go there. Don't forget," she told him, "we will see each other again and I'll know who you are right away!" It was decided that PK would help from the Kingdom of Light for several years before she made her journey into the Kingdom of Opposites.

"I won't forget you, PK, you know that." Gi assured her with a hug.

With his Guardian Angee by his side, it was time for the Prince to leave. He smiled at his family and his two best friends, Joni and Trevori, who were also making their final preparations to make their entrance, and with a wave of the King's hand, his son went through a thin veil and disappeared to appear on the other side as a newborn baby.

When the Prince emerged on the other side, he let out a big cry. "It's cold here," he thought and then heard this awful noise, "What is that? Is that coming from me?" He saw faces around him that he did not recognize and again he heard that awful noise that seemed to be coming from him.

Then he stopped. He saw the King and Queen, his sister PK, his Guardian Angee, and many other Angees and they were all applauding and laughing. He started to laugh, too. "I'm here," he thought, and he noticed that the awful noise stopped and he could hear himself laughing.

Then he heard another voice, "It's a beautiful baby boy and look, he's smiling!" Then he felt warm arms around him and looked up into the eyes of his new mother and saw his new father standing next to her.

He heard his new father say, "His voice is strong; I think he's going to be a singer." He then heard the soft voice of his new mother and she said, "He looks like a handsome prince."

He started to speak but it sounded different. Then he heard the Queen gently say to him, "They cannot understand you yet, but they will." The Royal Family stayed for a little while as they watched Gi's new parents fuss over him and talk about how beautiful he looked; then they waved goodbye for now and Gi fell asleep.

As promised, PK came every day to watch her brother as he ate, slept, and was held by his parents. He could see her and clapped his tiny hands together whenever she came to see him. He talked to her and she understood what he was saying, even though his parents just thought he was making baby noises.

Gi's friends made their appearance on the other side of the thin veil, just a few months later.

Soon it was time for PK's friends to leave. It was decided that Shajula would leave first, followed by Brilola, and then PK would be the last. The three friends spent a lot of time together in the field of flowers making promises that they would recognize each other when it was time to meet. They decided that when they saw a butterfly in the smaller kingdom, they would remember their time here and the promises they had made.

Then it was Shajula's turn to choose her family. The father she chose was a kind and loving being who owned a successful business that took him all over the kingdom. The mother was a beauty queen and loved to dance. They traveled together on business trips, saw many different places, met different beings, and the mother dressed in beautiful clothes. When they returned from their travels, they lived in a beautiful home on the lake and entertained many friends. They stopped traveling together when their son was born. The mother adored her son and stayed home to take care of him while the father traveled alone.

Shajula knew that she would learn a lot from both these beings and she left to begin her journey. The other two friends were there when Shajula made her appearance on the other side, letting out a loud cry just as Gi did, but then Shajula saw her friends and she smiled at them clapping her tiny hands. The friends visited her often and watched her grow. "When you see a butterfly," they told her, "you will think of us, and remember, 'Be the Light.'"

Brilola chose a family that already had a son and daughter. The father was a carpenter and made beautiful wood carvings. The mother was a baker who owned a small bakery shop where she made breads and cakes. Brilola knew that she would learn a lot from these two beings and she could also share what she already knew about art and beauty.

When Brilola made her entrance into the smaller kingdom, PK was there, smiling at her and reminding her about the butterfly. She visited her two friends and her brother Gi and his two friends every day reminding them, "Be the Light."

PK had already decided that she wanted to be close to her brother and the King and Queen were pleased with her decision. The mother she had chosen was the sister of Gi's mother. She was an artist and the father was a veterinarian. They lived in a big house and they had horses, but it would be several years before they would start a family.

She watched as her future father cared for the horses and nursed other animals and she knew she would learn a lot from him. She watched as her future mother studied art and painted beautiful pictures.

She visited the horses and was especially happy when she saw a field of sunflowers in this place. "Yes," she told the King and Queen, "I will begin my mission there."

PK continued with her lessons from the Medicine and Art Talent Experts and she helped those beings in the smaller kingdom when they requested help. She watched as the Angees sped to deliver the messages. PK was helping from her side.

She also spent a lot of time with the King and Queen as they talked about her mission. She continued to watch over Gi and her friends as they started to learn to walk and talk. Then it was time for PK to pass through the thin veil.

With her Guardian Angee by her side and surrounded by many Angees, she was ready to make her entrance. The King and Queen smiled proudly at their courageous daughter knowing that she would indeed bring Light into the smaller kingdom. She kissed them goodbye and waved goodbye, "I'll see you on the other side," she said smiling at them.

PK felt the shock of the cold when she made her entrance and she also let out a loud cry like all the others did. Then she saw her beloved King and Queen and she smiled. Her Guardian Angee and the other Angees were laughing and applauding.

PK felt the arms of her new mother wrapped around her and she heard her say, "You are a welcomed surprise, princess."

Her new father said "Welcome, Little One."

The King and the Queen laughed. Just then a butterfly flew by and everyone wondered how a butterfly came to be in the room. At the same time, somewhere in another town and in another city, a butterfly landed on a doll that Brilola was playing with and Shajula saw a butterfly as she was playing with her brother on the lake. She started to laugh and went chasing the butterfly. Both friends instantly knew, "PK is here!" The three friends would end up in the same town and become close friends again.

The Royal children and their friends had begun their journey. There would be many hills and valleys on the path that they would each have to climb. They would come face to face with the shadow of fear in the many twists and turns on the journey.

They would each experience their fear in their pain and suffering. There would be grief, disappointment, anger, sadness, and health problems. There would also be many moments of magic just when they need them the most. In those moments, they would each feel the presence of others helping and guiding them.

They would all meet again and they would instantly become friends as if they have known each other before in another time.

Each one would question, "Who am I? Why am I here? What is the purpose of my life?" Then they would finally get the answer from within; in the stillness and the quiet they would hear the voice of the King, "You are the children of Light. Be the Light."

Part III

⌦ Light Partners ⌧

KAREN AND BRIAN SMILED at the grandchildren as their story ended. Jo and Lee applauded. They had enjoyed the story. Then they all started talking at the same time, firing questions at the grandparents. "Do we really choose our parents?" "Will we really recognize our friends from the Kingdom of Light?" "I don't know what my talents are; when will they show up?" Karen and Brian answered their questions and after the excitement quieted down, everyone prepared to go to their assigned sleeping rooms.

They had become different people that weekend. They felt they had an important mission—even the two young girls understood how special they were. The cousins made a pact to keep in touch and remind each other to "Be the Light."

The legacy was now passed on. The birthday weekend was a roaring success! That night as Karen and Brian drifted off to sleep, the flowers on their nightstands were glowing such brilliant colors that they filled the entire house and touched the sleeping beings.

The next morning the whole household was in a flurry of activity as every grandchild was talking about the wonderful dreams they had. They were all given glimpses of the Kingdom of Light in their dreams. They rambled on and on about the different colors of light they saw in their dream and how everyone was filled with lights that moved when they moved. Everyone had a similar dream. There was excitement and electricity at the breakfast table.

Shane, always clowning around, had to ask his grandmother, "So, Grandma, you are PK in that story, aren't you, and Uncle Brian is the Prince?"

Before either grandparent could answer his question, Shane quickly said, as if afraid to hear the answer he already knew in his heart, "Aw, that's okay, you don't need to tell us, because I already know that I am of royalty anyway."

Nigel jumped in and said, "Does that mean I'm kind of like a prince?" Everyone laughed.

Karen said, "Well, the young ladies in your life already think you're a prince." Everyone laughed again.

Brian said, "The knowledge of the Kingdom of Light did not come to us until very recently, but the knowledge that we have a mission here is something that we have always known. We all have a mission and we all have talents to share with others to make our lives easier and brighter."

As the grandchildren listened to Brian's words, Karen said, "The most important thing we wanted to share with all of you in this reunion, other than my birthday cake, is to use your gifts and talents and "Be the Light" in this world. Your Light is brighter than 1,000 suns, and it can reach so many others when you share your chosen talents. Will you all promise us that you will remember to do this?"

After the children promised to do this, they all started talking again about how they were going to do this. The grandparents suggested that the grandchildren become Light Partners for each other. Karen explained, "Choose a Light Partner who will always be there to remind you of your mission to be a light here. There will be many times on this journey that you will attract the Shadow, and it's up to your Light Partner to help you get through that and find your way to your inner Light. Your Light Partner will also remind you to use and share your gifts and talents with the other Light Beings here."

The cousins instantly knew who their Light Partner would be. Kay and Shane, Nigel and Corina, and of course Jo and Lee had chosen each other with the older cousins promising to set the examples for the two younger girls.

Brian explained, "You are now the keepers of knowledge and you too will pass it on when the time is right." After many hugs and kisses and promises to keep in touch and "Be the Light" all the grandchildren finally left the beach house.

☞ A New Mountaintop ☜

KAREN HELPED BRIAN CLEAN up and they talked about their grandchildren with pride and joy.

Brian said, "I have one more birthday surprise for you, K, and we are going there now."

Karen noticed that Brian was packing a picnic basket of leftovers and asked, "Are we going on a picnic?"

Brian said with a twinkling in his eyes, "You'll see, PK; come on, let's go."

The two cousins got into Brian's car. Brian did not offer any hints on the birthday surprise as they enjoyed their 30-minute drive. Brian drove up a scenic mountain road and he said, "I discovered this place a few years ago when I was hiking and I wanted to share it with you."

Brian parked in what seemed like a secluded place surrounded by magnificent oak trees. He carried the picnic basket, took a couple of folding chairs and a blanket out of the truck, and together they walked for 10 minutes until they came upon a clearing and found themselves overlooking a spectacular panoramic view of the valley and the ocean below.

Karen exclaimed, "Wow! This view is breathtaking."

Brian set up the chairs and spread the blanket over a grassy spot. Karen joined him. They were both quiet as they settled in their chairs and enjoyed the view before them.

"The mountaintop," Karen whispered.

"Yes, the mountaintop," Brian said quietly, almost reverently. They talked about what it must have been like on their first mountaintop, high up above the clouds, and their first glimpse of the smaller kingdom. They talked about the lessons that the King and Queen imparted and they talked about their journey and all the twists and turns and the hills and valleys that they had crossed and climbed. They laughed as they recalled how they allowed the Shadow, the fear, to come into their lives during those times and how it disappeared when help arrived just in time to get them out of trouble.

They ate their lunch after they settled onto the blanket on the grassy ground. They talked about those family members who had completed their journeys and wondered if they truly accomplished what they had set out to do. Karen and Brian talked about their parents and why they had chosen them and how much they did learn from them.

They talked about their friends, Trevor, Jonathan, Shasha, and Lola. They agreed that their friends had accomplished what they had set out to do.

Trevor became an engineer for a large firm and did help design his gadgets as well as other things until he retired and he and Lola came to La Hacienda to help Shasha operate the business. He still continued to make others laugh, so his dream to bring laughter into many lives was also fulfilled.

They talked about how Jonathan's political career led him into the political arena where he was now a senator, respected among his peers and his constituents as a champion for the environment. He and his wife, Tracey, now lived in Washington D.C. and they often flew to California to see their daughter Noell and her family. On these visits, Jonathan and Tracey always took the time to visit with Brian.

Lola expanded her artistic talents into her well-known creative culinary skills and was not only the chef at La Hacienda but she had passed her talents on to her son, Bill, who had become well-known in his own right for his own culinary creative genius. Trevor and Lola's two granddaughters often graced La Hacienda with their visits and would always be there when their parents made their annual appearance. Everyone at La Hacienda enjoyed the culinary treats of their chef and her son.

Shasha certainly accomplished her mission to bring beauty into the world with her fashions and by bringing joy to the women who wear them. She not only did this but was also a well-known contributor to many charities. She had brought Light into many lives. Even though she'd had four husbands, she was still friends with all of them and she continued to dote on her two sons, Gordon and Zack from her first marriage. They had given her three talented and loving grandchildren and they also came to La Hacienda quite often to visit their still famous grandmother.

They talked about how Shasha's annual Christmas parties always included all of them and throughout the years, the six friends reunited at these parties. The cousins shared many delightful stories of their journey with their friends.

Karen teased Brian and said, "By the way, Brian, Shasha is still looking for her Prince Charming. What do you say, you come forward and announce yourself?"

Brian smiled thinking of Shasha, who had been his friend as well for many years. "She is still a looker, isn't she?"

The two had already previously agreed that they would not pass on the information about the Kingdom of Light to their friends. They would wait until the book was published so their friends could read it and see how much of it they could recall or were allowed to remember.

Karen wondered how she did not recall her husband Spencer in her recollection of the Kingdom of Light and concluded, "I think we were shown just enough to pass on to our grandchildren, so we will remind them of their mission. We made a pact to pass the knowledge of the inner Light to the beings who have chosen us."

Brian thought for a while and finally said, "I know that there is more to our growing up and learning about our original home than what we were shown, but I don't think it's only so we can pass it on to our grandchildren. Think about it, K; why do you think all this has been revealed to the both of us? I know that we both said it was so that we could pass it on to our grandchildren, but I think it's more than that. There is a bigger reason why we have been shown this; don't you agree?"

Karen said quietly, "Maybe it's just to comfort us and to remind us that we are never alone on our journey."

Karen felt the solitary tear roll down her cheek. Brian looked at her and said, "K, are you sad?"

"No, Brian, just happy to be here with you. We've been through so much together from our beginnings to now and I want you to know that I love you so much. My journey would not be the same if you hadn't been here with me through the bad and the good, the Light and the Shadow, the many hills and valleys."

Brian reached for his cousin's hand and gently squeezed it, "You've been there for me too, K." and he also felt tears well up in his eyes.

Brian put his arm around his cousin and she leaned against his shoulder as they both watched the view from their mountaintop. Anyone watching them could see the closeness they shared.

Before they left their new mountaintop, Brian reached into his pocket and handed Karen her birthday gift. Karen opened the gift and found, nestled in the jewelry box, a beautiful silver chain with a winged horse pendant. This time, the tears did flow as she ran her finger over her new treasure. Brian helped her put it on and she gave him a hug as she wiped her tears. It truly was a beautiful gift.

On her drive home, she considered calling her own children to let them know how the weekend went but decided that she'd let the grandchildren tell them. She smiled to herself and said aloud, this time knowing exactly who she was talking to, "Thank you for a wonderful weekend. The seeds are planted and I know they will grow into fruition."

She arrived home and called La Hacienda to let her friends know that she was back. She had received a message from Gail that the book would be ready before Christmas. Karen called Gail with additional changes she wanted on the inside cover.

Karen then called her friend David at the reservation and agreed to meet with him the next day after her consultation time with Scott. David was always such a happy distraction.

At dinner that evening, Shasha gave Karen an exquisite brooch of multiple translucent colors. Lola gave her a shawl with an angel design so that when she was wearing it, the wings of the angels spread to cover her shoulders. They were beautiful gifts, and with Brian's winged horse pendant around her neck, Lola's angel wings shawl wrapped around her, and Shasha's brooch with glimmering lights, it was the perfect birthday.

Karen looked at her friends through tear-filled eyes and said, "Thank you for this and thank you for always being my friends." They hugged each other and before they all got to crying, Shasha quickly changed the subject and they immediately discussed the final plans for Shasha's annual Christmas party. Jonathan and his wife Tracey had already said they would come and Brian always stayed over at Karen's after partying with his friends.

The rest of week, Karen spent a lot of time in her field of flowers, thinking of all that had happened in her life up to this moment. She remembered her recent visits with her two doctor friends, Scott and David. She smiled thinking of all that they had done as doctors to bring Light into this world of pain and suffering. She remembered feeling sad and helpless when confronted with those patients who could not be helped, but knowing what she now knew, she no longer felt sad for those patients because she knew that they were being called to return to the Kingdom of Light.

She thought of her wonderful parents and all that they had taught her to be and to do. She smiled thinking of them being in the Kingdom of Light now. She then turned her attention to Spencer, and now that she knew where he was, she also smiled.

She laughed to herself as she looked out at her small garden and realized now why she lovingly called it her field of flowers. She saw a couple of butterflies flying over her garden and now she could hear the music from the trees and flowers very clearly.

She glanced over at the empty chair next to her and softly said, "This has been a wonderful life."

⌒ The Journey Ends ⌒

THE FOLLOWING WEEK WAS Thanksgiving and Karen and Brian spent the day with their respective families. Karen, surrounded by her two children and their families, thought it was a festive occasion at Rosemarie's home.

Karen looked at Elaine and Rosemarie and remembered those days when they were children. They were beautiful girls, playful and loving. She remembered their time going through puberty, and the many times when they would argue with Karen, which gave her many anxious moments and sleepless nights.

She watched them now, grown into beautiful, successful women and wonderful mothers. Karen knew that they chose her to be their mother and wondered if they learned what they wanted to learn from her. She hoped so. She felt loved and blessed for having them on this journey and she was especially grateful for the grandchildren they had given her.

Little did Karen know that at that same moment, Brian was also watching his son, Chase, and was wondering the very same thing. Did he learn what he wanted to learn from the father he chose? Brian also felt blessed and grateful for the gifts of his two granddaughters, Corina and Jo.

The grandchildren had kept both Brian and Karen updated on the changes they'd made since last weekend and on what they'd do to be the Light in the world. Their parents remarked about the changes in their children after that birthday weekend. They seemed more serious about what they wanted to do or what they wanted to be, and yet at the same time they seemed happier. All they would say about their time at the reunion was that it was the best time they'd had and they now had a mission.

Kay had three days left of her school break and invited herself to spend those days with her grandmother. Karen gladly agreed to have her oldest grandchild with her.

That Sunday was the annual fundraiser drive at Karen's church and she thought Kay could help her go through the things in her cottage that she no longer used or needed so that she could contribute them to the drive.

After the wonderful Thanksgiving dinner, Karen and Kay left for the cottage but made a short detour to stop at La Hacienda to indulge in Lola's scrumptious

Thanksgiving desserts. Stuffed and happy, they continued on to the cottage and stayed up talking like two young girls at a slumber party until they couldn't keep their eyes open any longer.

The next day, Karen and Kay went through the cottage getting things ready for pickup for the church drive. Karen also gave Kay a couple of furniture pieces that Kay wanted for her apartment. By the time they were done, the cottage looked very roomy. There were other keepsakes that Karen wanted to give to the rest of her grandchildren, and she included Brian's grandchildren in the treasure giving. Kay agreed that she would make sure they got them.

It was mid-afternoon by the time they were done, and they devoured the lunch that Lola had sent over to them. Karen asked Kay to prepare the tea to bring out to the garden.

Kay was pleasantly surprised as she saw her grandmother gingerly piling strawberry ice cream onto two cones. "Hurry with the tea, before this ice cream melts all over my hands!" Karen instructed, as she made her way to her field of flowers.

Kay laughingly followed and after she placed the two cups of tea on the table between them, she gladly took one of the cones from her grandmother.

Karen was slowly enjoying her ice cream cone and said, "Strawberry ice cream is one of the simple pleasures of life that must be savored slowly," eyeing her granddaughter who was eating hers with record speed. They laughed.

After their ice cream time together, Karen told Kay about the afternoon when the Kingdom of Light revealed itself to her.

Karen began, "I met with my doctor that day not for a consultation on one of his patients' charts, but it turned out that the patient was me. It seems as if I have this rare disease that I've had since childhood, and it is very slowly but surely spreading throughout my body. We discovered it only a few months ago, and the prognosis is not good. Kay, I am dying."

She saw the shocked look on her granddaughter's face, but before Kay could say anything, Karen raised her hand indicating that Kay needed to let her finish. "No, there is nothing they can do, Kay. My journey is nearing an end. I left my doctor's office that day feeling sorry for myself, and that was when I heard the music coming from the trees at the nearby park. I followed the music and sure enough, it was coming from the branches. I'd never heard it before, although, I am sure that your Uncle Brian heard it all his life. I came here to my garden that I call my field of flowers. I never understood why I always called this little garden a field of flowers, but by the end of that afternoon, I understood."

Karen told Kay about the apparitions that appeared before the vision of the Kingdom of Light came to her. She also told her about discovering the magical glowing flowers on her lap. Kay was crying and Karen reached out and squeezed her granddaughter's hand.

"I wanted to tell you and the other grandchildren about that vision so you can begin to truly understand why you are all here. I was shown that at the end of my life, but now you and the others have a whole lifetime ahead of you to follow your passions, and those will lead you to the mission you came here to do."

When Kay asked why she didn't tell anyone about her sickness. Karen smiled and said, "Precisely for the reason that they will cry just like you are doing now and this is not how I want to see you and everyone else in my last few weeks. I want to create memories with you and the others so you can spend the last few moments with me, laughing, sharing, and eating strawberry ice cream.

"Wipe your tears, dear, we have been given a glimpse of what all this is about. It is not about crying, feeling sorry for yourself and for me; it's about celebrating your life and my life. Do you not see that now?"

Kay nodded and she obediently wiped her tears. She understood what her wise grandmother was saying, but when she thought about not seeing her again, the tears threatened to spill over. Karen watched her closely, knowing that she was trying to summon all her courage not to cry again.

"There are some things I need for you to do for me so you need to pay attention, all right?" Kay nodded.

Karen told Kay that because she was the oldest and the only one privy to this information, she must be the one who needed to hold everything together when the time came. Kay promised her grandmother that she would.

Karen said, "I think that it will be you, my other grandchildren, and your cousins who will be the ones to teach the others to celebrate my life instead of grieving for me. You and Shane must explain this to your mothers.

"Kay, I feel that your Uncle Brian will really take this hard. I've thought about sharing this with him, but I just couldn't bring myself to tell him, because he will spend precious time trying to convince me to take tests and more tests and second opinions and so on, and that is not how I want to spend my last few days here. I just want him and all of you to remember that birthday weekend."

Kay understood what her grandmother was now saying and assured her, "I will be there for Uncle Brian if he needs me."

Karen told Kay about the book about the Kingdom of Light that was supposed to be published by Christmas and its purpose—to leave the legacy behind for children, grandchildren, and all the generations to come. Kay assured her grandmother that she would make sure that the book would be passed on.

Karen smiled. She knew that Kay truly understood. Her Light would continue to shine through the story and from beyond. Over the next couple of days, Karen and Kay spent a lot of time in the field of flowers, talking, laughing, and sometimes crying together. It was one of the best times they'd spent together. In the evenings, Kay accompanied her grandmother to La Hacienda where she was given the honor of joining Karen and her friends on the terrace for their evening meals and wine. A few times, Karen caught Kay surveying the loving bond of the three elder women with a look of sadness on her face. Karen would give her a wink and a smile, and Kay would smile back at her.

On the last afternoon of Kay's visit, the two sat enjoying the beautiful view of the lake and Kay looked at her grandmother and said, "I'll always remember our time here; this is truly a special place and when I get my own place, I'm going to have a field of flowers just like this one to remind me of the Kingdom of Light."

Karen reached over and squeezed her granddaughter's hand and said, "The field of flowers is always inside of you. It's the beauty you carry with you at all times. It is the beauty of who you are, my sweet girl."

Kay quietly said, "I'm going to miss you, G-ma."

Karen turned to look right into her granddaughter's eyes and said, "Kay, you can't get rid of me that easily. I'm not going away. I am always here with you, right here." Karen placed her hand over her granddaughter's heart.

Kay looked at her grandmother and said, "I know that I will always carry you in my heart, but you won't be here for me to talk to."

"Who says?" Karen asked gently, "Who says that you cannot talk to me? Because my tired and sick body isn't here? You know that I am not my body, you are not your body, we are beyond these temporary vehicles. My dear sweet girl, when I discard this body, I can be at home and here in this kingdom at the same time. You can talk to me any time. You'd better, because I'm going to be around to continue to guide you to your mission. I am going to continue to love and guide you from a place where I truly can. When you come to those twists and turns and hills and valleys and don't know where to turn and the Shadow seems to keep getting bigger and bigger around you, just go into that silent place, and you will feel my presence and hear my guidance."

Karen squeezed Kay's hand and leaned back and lovingly said, "Kay, when you grieve for me, you are bringing in the Shadow; don't grieve for me, celebrate my journey as I will celebrate yours until we reunite again. Wipe away those tears, dear sweet girl, and know always that I love you and I so appreciate you being in my life. Now, how about that tea?"

Kay hugged her grandmother and she quickly turned so she wouldn't see the tears in her eyes threatening to flow. She then went inside the house to refill their tea.

When Kay left, Karen felt a loving presence in the chair where Kay had been sitting a few moments earlier. She glanced over and saw the same three apparitions she saw that one afternoon. She smiled at her Guardian Angee and the King and Queen.

"It is time to go, Little One," the King announced in a gentle voice.

"I know, Father, and I am ready." Karen replied and smiled as she closed her eyes for the last time.

When Kay returned to the garden, her grandmother was gone. With the angel wings shawl wrapped around her shoulders, Karen looked like she was sleeping peacefully, but Kay knew the Angees had come and taken her away.

Kay kneeled down, hugged her grandmother and whispered her goodbye. She cried, then called her parents and her Uncle Brian and La Hacienda.

Trevor, Lola, and Shasha rushed over to the cottage, shocked at the news that Karen had passed on. Trevor carried her body to her bedroom with the angel wings shawl around her and waited for the others to arrive.

Trevor was consoling his wife and Shasha. Everyone was asking, "What happened? We just saw her a couple of hours ago, she looked fine. What happened? How did this happen?"

Kay told her grandmother's friends that her grandmother had known that she was dying. Kay shed a few tears but she was the calmest adult in that room. She understood that her grandmother's friends were in shock and tried to explain the best she could what her grandmother had shared with her the last few days.

"She told no one and she only told me about it two days ago. The only two people who knew of her illness were Dr. Scott and Dr. David, but there was only so much they could do. She didn't even say anything to her daughters or to Uncle Brian. She didn't say anything to you because she didn't want to spend her last few weeks crying with you, she wanted only to continue your time with her in laughter and good times," Kay calmly explained to the hysterical group around her.

Trevor, despite his shock at what happened, marveled at Kay's calmness and said, "Your grandmother told you that?"

"Yes, she did," Kay replied.

Lola and Shasha went into the bedroom to say their last goodbyes and Trevor continued to talk with Kay.

Shortly afterward, the family started arriving. Brian came in first. He lived an hour away but made it to the cottage in record time. He must have broken every speeding law on the freeway. He looked at everyone without a word and walked straight into his cousin's bedroom and held her in his arms and cried out, "NO! You can't take her now! How could you take her now? How could you? How could you?" he kept repeating as if talking to someone else in the room.

He was inconsolable. He kept crying out, "The mission is not complete. It's not complete, we've just begun. It's not complete. How could you? How could you take her now?" He was not making any sense to anyone, except to Kay.

Karen's daughters and the rest of the grandchildren arrived and Trevor had to pull Brian away from Karen so her children could see their mother.

Kay hugged her uncle but was unsuccessful in calming him down. He kept saying, "Why now? Why now?"

There was a lot of activity going on in the cottage as they awaited the arrival of the coroner to take the body away. Everyone was in shock, crying, and asking the same questions, "How?", "When?", and "Why?"

Kay again explained what her grandmother shared with her. The only ones who seemed to be calmed by this were the grandchildren. They now realized why she wanted them all together that last birthday weekend.

Shane and Kay found Brian in the garden, weeping uncontrollably sitting in Karen's favorite chair. "Why didn't she tell me, Kay? We tell each other everything; we were best friends. Why didn't she tell me about her illness?"

After he calmed down, Kay quietly explained what Karen shared with her the last few days they were together.

Brian broke down again in uncontrollable tears and the kids left him in his sorrow.

Brian leaned back in the chair, looked up at the stars and thought of the last time he saw his cousin on their "new mountaintop" and he recalled all they talked about that day. *She knew then, of course she knew then, why didn't she say anything?* He recalled what she said, "Maybe it's only to comfort us and remind us that we are never alone on our journey." He also remembered seeing a tear roll down her cheek when she said it. *Oh, K, how can I make it without you now?*

He finally went back into the cottage and composed himself as much as he could. The coroner had come and gone. His nieces, Elaine and Rosemarie, were telling him about funeral arrangements and he only listened halfheartedly. He noticed that Karen's grandchildren were watching him as if to get their cue from him, but all he could do was hug each one.

He left with Trevor and they headed to La Hacienda where Brian would spend the night. Shasha and Lola stayed and talked with Karen's family about the plans and the calls that needed to be made.

That night when everyone was asleep, the bouquet of flowers glowed. It glowed and filled Karen's empty bedroom in the cottage, it glowed and filled Shasha and Lola's rooms, and it also glowed brightly and filled the beach house even though Brian wasn't there. Brian, after sharing a bottle of brandy with Trevor, was sound asleep in one of the empty bedrooms at La Hacienda.

⌒ Saying Goodbye ⌒

BRIAN MOVED THROUGH THE next few days as if
in a fog. He didn't remember grieving for his parents this way. The pain of Karen's death seared through
him like a burning knife. He was depressed. Nothing
anyone could say could make him snap out of it. He
made it to the funeral and mustered as much compo-
sure as he could.

At the funeral were many of Karen's friends who he
knew and Jonathan and Tracey were also there. Brian
did get a chance to speak to Scott and listened as Scott
explained that Karen was adamant about not being in
the hospital for her last few days. David, her shaman
doctor friend, explained that he had given Karen herb
mixtures to take and this helped her ease the pain.

"She was in good spirits last week when she came
to see me." he said. "I wish I could have done more,
but the illness had been in her body since she was born,
and it slowly, over the years, poisoned her system. It

was one of those rare diseases that we were not able to detect until it was too late to reverse it.

"This happening now is so unfortunate, Brian, because I just received word that Karen is being honored for her research contribution to the cure of blindness. Karen had worked so many years on convincing the medical professional that the mixture of herbs we've come up with should be a part of the treatment for blindness and now that they've finally agreed, Karen is not here to be recognized for her work on the cure."

Brian knew how much time Karen had spent on the research for this form of complementary medicine and how frustrated she had been when the testimonials of its success had fallen on deaf ears. Now after all these years and hundreds of successes, they were paying attention.

David told Brian that he'd let him know when the event would take place and he hoped that Brian, who was the first recipient of this complementary medicine, would be there on behalf of Karen. Brian agreed. *She was always there for me when I received my accolades. Now it's her turn and she's gone.*

Brian was so engrossed in his thoughts that he didn't hear any part of the memorial service. Afterward, everyone was invited to La Hacienda for refreshments.

When most of Karen's friends left, Gail took Brian aside and said, "Brian, she called me a few days ago and faxed me several pages that were handwritten and she wanted me to insert them in a few copies of the book. I didn't understand then why she wanted me to do this when it would have been more economical if she personally signed them after the book was printed, but now I understand why. It's as if she knew that she would not make it to see the publication. I brought the books with me that have the special pages inserted."

Gail then handed the newly published book, *Be the Light*, to Brian. Brian looked at the book and again he felt himself ready to cry. He excused himself from Gail and walked away with book in hand. Gail watched as Brian walked away feeling her own tears on her face again. *This is so hard for him.*

Karen's grandchildren and Brian's two granddaughters gathered together and talked about the birthday weekend and the legacy that Karen passed on to them. They talked about Karen now being in the Kingdom of Light watching over them. They were not as sad as most of the people there. "They don't understand like we do," they said to each other.

Gail found the rest of them on the terrace and she proceeded to hand each one of them Karen's book. Each had a personally inscribed message from Karen. Each book was addressed to each grandchild with an inscription that read, *I'll be guiding you from this side. Remember, "Be the Light" for this world.*

For the books to Shasha and Lola, Karen wrote, *I'll be waiting for you in the field of flowers with the butterflies.*

Karen also left a letter that she had written earlier in the week for each one of her friends. She thanked them for being her friend in this kingdom and the kingdom before this one. *After you read the book, you'll know, just as I did just a few weeks ago,* she wrote.

For the books for Jonathan and Trevor, she wrote, *Remember our mission.*

For the books to her daughters, Elaine and Rosemarie, and to Brian's son, Chase, she wrote, *Thank you for the grandchildren. Behold their Light.*

She also left a letter for both of her daughters in which she thanked them for choosing her as their mother and hoped that she had taught each one of them what they needed to learn on the journey of life.

Elaine and Rosemarie cried and held each other trying to find comfort in each other, but it was their children who gave them the greatest comfort in their calmness and acceptance.

Gail left and those who remained sat down and proceeded to read Karen's book. Shasha, Lola, Jonathan, and Trevor began to cry again. Elaine, Rosemarie, and Chase did the same thing. They were beginning to understand who had been in their midst all this time, the Princess of the Kingdom of Light herself.

Then they heard laughter coming from the terrace. The grandchildren were laughing. They went out to see what was going on, and there they saw several butterflies of different colors flying around, and soon everyone else started laughing too. PK was definitely letting them know that she was well and happy in the Kingdom of Light. A sad day turned into laughter and more tears mixed with the laughter. The grandchildren began singing, "This little light of mine, I'm going to let it shine, let it shine, let it shine, let it shine." Everyone was soon laughing and crying at the same time.

The Power of Love

BRIAN WAS NOT A part of the group at La Hacienda. He didn't see the butterflies. He didn't hear the laughter of the grandchildren. He had left right after Gail handed him his book.

Brian was sitting on a blanket on the grassy mountaintop asking the same question, "Why?" His heart had been breaking the last few days, and things were beginning to take their toll. Brian was exhausted and felt himself getting sleepy. He heard the music coming from the oak trees and he let the music soothe him to sleep as he wrapped his arms around his legs and put his head down.

The Angees were all around him shining their light on him. He felt their presence but was too tired to look up. Again, he sleepily asked, "Why take her now? We just found the truth about each other."

Brian felt himself spinning into a vortex of vibrating colors and then it stopped and he saw a scene play out before him.

Brian was three years old playing in his father's boat while his father was tinkering around with the engine. When his father was finished with his work, he reached to pick up Brian, ready to take him home, but just then an explosion came and Brian and his father went flying into the air.

Brian saw his Guardian Angee and his father's Guardian Angee come swooping down to catch them in midair and slowly and gently carry them to the shore. The boat went up in flames.

He saw PK's horrified expression watching the scene from the other side of the veil. He then saw her appear on his side calling his name, "Gi!" No one else could see her. The sounds of sirens filled the air and Brian and his father were taken into an ambulance. The Guardian Angees and PK were with them in the ambulance.

In the next scene, Brian had bandages around his eyes and his father had a cast on his leg. Brian's father had broken his leg and Brian had small fragments of metal lodged in both his eyes. He saw a scene of a doc- tor telling his parents that he was blind in one eye and the other eye would also lose its vision. He would even- tually become totally blind.

He saw PK standing by saying, "No, no, he needs to see. He must see the beauty and the Light. No, no, you can cure him."

Brian saw his parents cry and console each other and his father blame himself for his negligence. He saw his parents pray for their son to receive his sight. He saw Angees surrounding his parents. He saw the Medical Experts from the Kingdom of Light giving instructions to the Angees to tell the doctor what needed to be done to save Gi's eyes. He saw that the doctor was not listening to the whispers.

He saw and heard PK plead with the King and Queen to send her in. "I know what needs to be done; I need to go there now. We cannot wait; he'll lose his eyesight. He won't grow to see the dolphins."

The Queen was patiently explaining that it was not time for PK to go. She was not to leave for another ten years. "No. No. It will be too late. I can't help from here if the doctor is not listening to what we are sending."

Brian watched as PK stood by his side while he was at the hospital and she stayed with him when his parents took him home. He knew that he, little Brian, couldn't see her anymore; all he saw was darkness with the bandages on his eyes. He was crying, demanding "Where is the light?" and only PK understood what he was saying. She kept telling him, "I'm here, Gi. I'm right here." Brian reached up his little arms but could not see anything and again he cried and cried.

The King and Queen watched their children and watched the sister reaching out to the brother. They finally gave in to PK's demands to let her start her journey now. As PK was being prepared for her journey to enter the smaller kingdom, much to the surprise of her chosen mother, the King and Queen took PK to the mountaintop and explained what she would need to give up to make this journey now. PK didn't care what the sacrifice was, as long as she could get there right away. So, the Royal Family made the pact.

The King and Queen would show the doctors here how to slow down the deterioration of Gi's one good eye until PK could complete her growth to help him. In exchange for coming to the smaller kingdom much earlier than originally agreed upon, PK would return to the Kingdom of Light much earlier.

The King explained to the Princess that there is order in the balance of both kingdoms and that is why her earlier entrance meant an earlier departure. PK agreed.

PK showed up in Brian's life by the time he was four years old. When she saw him for the first time in the smaller kingdom, she immediately placed her stubby hands over his eyes and uttered, "Gi. Gi." Both mothers thought she was saying "Glee, Glee."

In the next scene, Brian saw the King and Queen smiling lovingly at him and they said, "That is why she was called to return home. Time is the most precious commodity on your journey and your sister loved you so much that she was willing to give up her time there to get to you on time. It is that kind of love where that magical Light connects both kingdoms and its powers move events and situations in both kingdoms. Her main mission was to help you 'see the Light' in that world. The last part of her mission was to let you 'see the Light' of this place by sharing the vision she was given. That opened you up to see where you both came from. So you have seen the Light of the smaller kingdom and the Light of this kingdom. Her mission was complete.

"There is an underlying order to everything that happens. This is what creates balance and harmony in both kingdoms. You must now let your sister's Light fill this kingdom. She is no longer there to 'Be the Light,' so this is what you now must do. 'Be the Light' for her. Your sadness is creating more Shadow around you. Break through that Shadow and be the brightest Light you can be for both of you. We are always here. You are never alone. Finish your journey, complete your mission, and rejoin us when you are done."

Brian woke up and finally he understood the whys. Hugging his knees with his head buried in them, he cried for the last time sitting there on the mountaintop and felt PK's love from the depths of his being filling him up.

Karen, Karen, you gave up so much for me. A slight breeze came up and he knew those were the Angees' wings going by. They were surrounding him and holding the light of the vision he had just witnessed. When he lifted his head, he saw a butterfly sitting on his hand.

The butterfly fluttered away and landed on Karen's book next to him. He watched the butterfly flutter away and as it did, the book opened to the dedication page and Brian saw for the first time her inscription, *I will be loving you from this side and I'll be at the mountain-top waiting for you.*

He looked up then and saw before him the most spectacular sunset he had ever seen. At that exact moment, everyone at La Hacienda witnessed the same scene from the terrace. They had just finished reading the book. They were applauding the sunset and the dozens of beautiful butterflies that appeared on the terrace.

Brian burst out in laughter. He stood up with his arms up in the air, yelling at the top of his lungs, "Yes! I love you PK. I'll be the Light for both of us, for our grandchildren, our children, and for all who read your words. Yes! The Princess has come and she has spoken! Now the Prince is awake! Look out, world, I'm here to spread my Light to every corner!" He thought, *how utterly and profoundly simple it all is,* and started laughing again.

At that exact moment, in the Kingdom of Light, Wings, carrying PK, was landing on their first mountaintop. Her arms were also raised up high, one holding her giant paintbrush and one holding her palette of colors; she was laughing and the choir of Angees were singing.

About the Author

LIZ CRISOSTOMO is from the island of Guam, and currently lives in southern California and is a student of the Holmes Institute of Higher Consciousness. She is a spiritual counselor, a life coach, an artist as well as a holistic health practitioner.

A grandmother of seven and a Religious Science Practitioner, she conducts workshops and teaches the spiritual principles of daily living. She started a women's group called Women of Wisdom, a gathering of women who come together to explore and embrace the divine feminine within. She inspires and empowers women to connect to the light of their feminine divinity and bring their light into their homes, communities, and the world.

Her published works include poems and magazine articles.

www.ingramcontent.com/pod-product-compliance
Lightning Source LLC
Chambersburg PA
CBHW032147020726
47496CB00003B/751